The Meekness of Isaac

BOOKS BY WILLIAM O'ROURKE

Nonfiction
The Harrisburg 7 and the New Catholic Left (1972)

Fiction
The Meekness of Isaac (1974)

The
Meekness
of
Isaac

A NOVEL

William O'Rourke

Thomas Y. Crowell Company
ESTABLISHED *1834*
NEW YORK

Designed by Ingrid Beckman

Manufactured in the United States of America

Library of Congress Cataloging in Publication Data

O'Rourke, William.
    The meekness of Isaac.

    I. Title.
PZ4.O748Mc [PS3565.R65]   813'.5'4   74-8372
ISBN 0-690-00299-8

            1   2   3   4   5   6   7   8   9   10

To

A. L. R.

*

J. A. R.

and their children

And Isaac spake unto Abraham
his father, and said, My father:
and he said, Here am I, my son.
And he said, Behold the fire and
the wood, but where is the lamb
for a burnt offering?

—Genesis 22:7

PROLOGUE

I HAVE something to disclose to you, but you must be wary of disclosures, for that is when someone thinks he is telling the truth about himself. As a child of the Middle West there was nothing to do but leave it, for it is the center of the country and any direction in which you may go is away. When I finally left, I had stayed on longer than I should; but a youth departs his hometown the way a snake quits its skin: A dry sheath of growing up remains behind.

The Meekness of Isaac

ONE

NEW YORK is the most human of cities, if only because it is a stranger to those who live within it. West End, above Seventy-second Street, is a broad avenue; no shops rust away the bottoms of the buildings. The sidewalks have few people on them and down each numbered street a park can be seen, stands of trees and a dash of river below the palisade of New Jersey. The wall of buildings on West End Avenue is a bulwark that shuts out Broadway's din.

There is no lease he needs to sign. A furnished room, a stunted icebox, a two-burner gas stove, a pipe with clogged sprinklers runs the length of the ceiling. Twenty-nine dollars a week.

"My, you're lucky to find this; places are hard to come by, now that schools are starting again. You'll have to tell me now, others want to look at it. Doesn't it have nice floors? A graduate student? Isn't that lovely; most of my people are Spanish, but I prefer students . . ."

She is pregnant. He is accustomed to being around term-swollen women.

A stone eagle spreads its wings over a scallop-shell pool. Green slat benches face the river. Beneath a retaining wall basketball courts and a children's playground; small boys run in and out of shacks; older youths practice foul shots. Baby carriages are pushed along asphalt pathways; the West Side Highway is linked with cars. Bundled old men and women on the benches read newspapers, shopping bags and dogs at their feet.

Leaves swirl in the fountain's dusky water. Brian Kilpatrick looks back up the street and picks out his room's bay window. He had no place to live and now he does; nothing seems difficult once done.

JAKE GRASS was four weeks out of the army, two weeks out of school, and one week into working with his father, selling hardware, and it was a manufacturers' convention that brought them to the city. Through the chambers of Pennsylvania Station flows a cellular streaming. Brian finds the gate from which he expects Jake and his father to emerge. A train debouches its passengers, but they were not among them. He climbs the stairs to the station's main hall and hears behind him, "There he is . . ."

Jake and Mr. Grass. They mumble greetings. Brian

shakes Jake's hand with both of his. For the three of them it is a reunion in a strange country. Mr. Grass is amused by the length of Brian's hair. Jake says: "Let's get to your place so I can change." Mr. Grass tells his son, "I'll meet you in the lobby of the Howard Johnson's at nine o'clock."

Jake's presence is a sudden windstorm that tears up all the worries that Brian had let put down roots.

1

Mail falls through the slot. Mrs. Grass rises, wipes her lips with a napkin and goes to fetch it.

"There's one from Jake," she says and drops the rest of the day's mail in front of her husband.

Jake's letter, page by page, is passed around the table. Following his salutation Jake had listed a column of numbers:

$$
\begin{array}{r}
31 \\
30 \\
31 \\
\underline{27} \\
119
\end{array}
$$

I'm at that stage of the game where I'm more restless than ever before—as you can see by the simple addition above— I've 119 days left. I've left the Third Platoon for the rear—the rear being LZ Baldy—about 10–15 miles south of

Da Nang—we've been rocketed a few times & a few mortar rounds drop in most every night, but I've got sandbag and wood walls around me about 4 feet thick, & about 3 feet thick roof, so there's no point in heading for the trench . . .

Brian looks up at what surrounds him: blooming dogwood trees, a late spring breeze through the large kitchen windows, lunch with Jake's mother and father.

Anyway, the kid's going to make it. Yes sir. I went to LZ Colt—about five miles N.W. of here to give the guys in my platoon some shots—they're something else—I didn't realize how much I care for them—I saw all the new pictures of wives, girls, kids, parents, etc. Caught all the latest gossip, heard in detail how the guys who got it got it . . .

As she reads, Mrs. Grass quarters an apple, cuts the seed saddle from a slice and hands the fruit to Brian, without looking away from the page. Her outstretched hand, the curved fourth of the apple, a dinghy bouyed up on the tips of her fingers.

. . . plus a few complaints from the men that their new medic isn't up to par (me) especially from the Soul Brothers, who tell me that he's not as casual as I am . . .

Each sheet of paper weighs as much as a memorial stone to Brian. Mr. Grass snaps a potato chip. An ambush trigger, Brian thinks.

. . . thanks for writing about Brian's arrest. I hate to think of his feelings—I'm not overly fond of the reservists—I'm glad I wasn't there & hope I'm never in that situation. It won't keep him out of the army though, he has to commit

some kind of felony, and I don't think he's ready for that . . .

"That's right, Brian," Mr. Grass says, after reading the passage aloud, "they won't mind one little arrest; they want you cause you're just the right size for those tunnels over there; you'll be a regular tunnel rat . . ."

He laughs, shaking the table. Its end rests on his belly.

Brian had protested to the Grasses the day the curfew that resulted in his arrest had begun. "The so-called riots began," he had fumed, "when that black high school started a march because of King's death; it was no more rowdy than a homecoming parade by one of the white south side schools; then after they gassed the black kids who assembled in front of City Hall, gassed them in the church basement, fires break out in the ghetto, the police go in and gleefully shoot a few spade cats, the National Guard is called in and the whole city is under a curfew. One day, the troops arrive, the whole city is controlled. At home, my family watches the news, the cops shooting at each other, my father saying they should kill all the black bastards. A week of curfew!"

The National Guardsmen had been called up from the small towns of Missouri. Their first trip to the Big City away from Neosho, Sedalia, Tarkio, Chillicothe, Boonville; called up from their jobs, saying good-bye to the wife, a squat sphinx in front of the full moon television. Goin' up to K.C. to quell the niggers.

The Grasses had sympathized with Brian, when he later

arrived in their kitchen with the announcement, "I've been arrested."

Driving home one night during the curfew he had been stopped at a barricade, yanked out of the family station wagon, legs splayed apart till the car was needed for support. Hands were run in haste over his body, roughly, in order to extinguish any charge of intimacy.

He was the only catch for the night in the Country Club district of the city and was handed down a shabby chain-of-command. First, the National Guardsmen, in stuffy khaki uniforms, smelling of hot canvas long packed away, the tents of his own Boy Scout past; then to a man driving a black sedan, a silver star painted on the door, a faceless badge, penny-arcade credentials and on to a colonel, with sparse hair, furrowed into a widow's peak. To each he repeated the same story: dinner at a friend's, just driving home, thought he'd be let through, he did not know the conduct of a curfew. He did not mention that he went on his way after the curfew started only because he had been unable to persuade the young woman into letting him remain the night.

The colonel left two privates guarding him, firing-squad fashion, pointing their rifles; the fixed bayonets were rusty. The colonel walked back up the street, a thoughtful lift to his chin, looking into the night sky, watching for flambeaus, the white tufts of parachutes, falling down to secure the city. Store windows were alight, expensive goods on tiny velvet platforms; they glitter like the eyes of nocturnal animals. A dark movie marquee tells the night its feature, *The Scalphunters.*

Brian was told to drive to another barricade and the Guardsmen got into the car's front seat with him, their bayonet-tipped weapons as awkward as large band instruments.

"You should have stayed where you were," one young Guardsman whispers to Brian.

At the barricade they climb out; the soldiers walk over to a loose formation of troops and settle into their collective shape. The city police are here. Tribal powers. The rent-a-guard appears and reports to the police like a neighboring pygmy. Jake's first letter from Vietnam is in Brian's shirt pocket. Soldiers here, soldiers there. He submits to a bloodless ritual acting out distant sacrifices.

In a paddy wagon Brian rides downtown with two others picked up elsewhere. One begins to slap his head against the steel webbing over the door window. Slap, repeatedly, slap: a discus thrower swinging back, two, three, four times. A waffle redness appears on his brow. The other takes him up in his arms; they remain a drab Pietà till the wagon reaches the Jackson County jail.

The police joke with one another. Locker-room banter after a game; won or lost, it didn't matter; they are off the field and are comfortable together.

The room is a combination of bus station, cheap eaterie,

flophouse, and failed bank. Behind teller bars a clerk frowns, listens to the information he has requested from Brian. University student, twenty-one, no previous arrests.

The man, a similar rooster-neck civil servant that had given Brian his Peace Corps application. That clerk had smiled.

Brian was released at dawn. The family station wagon had been impounded and he walked to a bus stop near Union Station. Nearby was his father's business. Main Street. A jeep patrols, a large machine gun mounted in the rear. Soldiers ride in it surrounded by concertina wire. Other cities had curfews, Brian knew, Washington, Detroit, Newark. It had been a spring of fear.

He waited for a southbound bus in the morning's mizzling weather, regretting the tedious explanations ahead. He would reach home just as his small brothers and sisters came looking for dyed eggs in the shadowy hiding places of the gray morning rooms. It was Easter Sunday.

THE TAPE *of Jenny's singing was real sweet; the guys that heard it thought it was someone famous; but I said, Naw, that's my little sister. Beautiful moon over here—a heat like you can't imagine during the day—sun hot, hot, hot—breeze at night.*

After rereading the letter, Mrs. Grass fixes a pot of coffee, returns and looks again at the last paragraph.

My moustache & Uncle Ho (lower lip whiskers) continue to grow, all thirty of them—but it's almost visible now. I'm rambling so I'd better close. Give my love to everyone who deserves it. I'm just biding my time. Subsequently, Jake.

She folds the letter, replaces it in its envelope. The waves of a postmark ripple over the word, *free.* It did not require a stamp since it had been sent from a combat zone. Sunken treasure, that *free,* Brian thought. Mr. Grass looks into the other mail, business correspondence, the weekly pale invoices sent to him.

"I'm going to have to make a trip to Des Moines soon," Mr. Grass says; then, "Can you imagine Jake with his 'Uncle Ho'? I hope he shaves it off before he gets home."

Jake's name, uncaged, flaps hecticly in the room.

"I'll pick up the kids and do some shopping," Mr. Grass says, winding his watch.

"Now, don't you and Kilpatrick get into any arguments while I'm gone," he says to his wife, at the sink, soapsuds braceleting her wrists. Brian and Mrs. Grass fought over the war daily in her kitchen.

Mr. Grass and Brian exchange smiles, wave good-bye. From the table Brian watches Mrs. Grass, the small kicks of her elbows at the sink while she scrapes off dishes. They rise on her left, Euclidian clusters.

"Get yourself some coffee, Brian; they're thick, powerful dregs . . . oh, here, I'll wait on you if that's what you want . . . you get more of my time than my own children, and more attention; they should get the service you receive—except they'd be spoiled; you're spoiled, Kilpatrick, sitting there, so easily miffed if I say anything that unsettles you."

Jake's letter sits in the middle of the table and they avoid it like a sleeping infant.

"The edge is on me today . . ."

She laughs at her rearrangement of the cliché, a thing she did; her hand rests lightly on Brian's shoulder. Moving to the end of the table she shakes out her children's laundered garments. Makes pant legs flat, smooths T-shirts; she puts bulky stacks into an oval wicker basket.

"Oh, these old legs can't take much more . . ."

She stretches out her right arm, a swimmer's stroke, across the table and rests her head on it.

"Do you think I'm starting to complain?" she asks Brian, looking up alertly, "I'm only talking back to the little pains. I never used to; I never used to talk back to anyone; wasn't proper. Years ago I had appendix trouble; it was too inflamed at the time to remove, too dangerous, so they only scraped it. For a while I had tubes in my nose, liquids flowing and ebbing, and a drain in my side. I was miserable. I couldn't even move in bed, was intolerant of noise. I *was* intolerant. I became annoyed with the colored nurses' helpers who were always singing in the halls, fooling with boyfriends; they'd come to move me or change the bedding and would seem to do it with more clumsiness than necessary. So I suffered and felt sorry for myself. As soon as the tubes were removed I was changed to a ward with maternity cases. The hospital was crowded and had to take the private room; so I felt myself resenting this. I was put next to a young woman who talked endlessly. Dyed blonde hair, she read movie magazines and when I wanted to just silently suffer she would chat on; she was having some problem getting released, her other children were staying with a friend who supposedly treated them badly; her husband had absconded or couldn't care. The girl was a Catholic though, and was saying prayers to speed her departure. I could feel myself never getting close to her; she would do things that I couldn't abide—cleaning between her toes with her fingers right before they brought in lunch, things like that. She finally led me into conversation about her son who she most worried over; I told her about Ned; when he died, so young he died in Holy Innocence and how Father Blade said he was an unnamed saint; so, if she wanted a saint to pray to she could use him. I finally got moved back to a semiprivate room and forgot about the girl, but a couple of days later she appeared in my room, packed and ready to leave, and wanted to thank me, saying she was leaving and she wanted me to know that she had prayed to my son and she was sure he was the saint who helped her . . ."

She turned away and went back to the sink. Ned, a son drowned in a water-filled construction ditch nearby a former home in Saint Louis. One day, arguing about the war, she had been especially agitated with Brian, who had been baiting her with his callow arrogance. She said then, shocking and silencing him, "I have lost one son and am prepared to lose another."

In the present ensuing lull, Brian went to pour himself more coffee; as he neared her, she brokenly said, "Oh, Brian, don't feel sorry for me, these are tears of happiness . . ."

Startled by her weeping, Brian shuffled, began to stammer.

"Don't let me scare you away, Kilpatrick," she said, holding a paper towel that she had dampened to her cheek, "they all should be home soon. You might want to leave me in tears, thinking I'd blush when we saw each other again, but I wouldn't, I wouldn't," she said, beginning to laugh at Brian's alarmed expression.

She returned to her ironing, the slap, slip, slide of the iron, the three sounds of surf on sand. Brian sat by her at the table reading a magazine. The afternoon recedes over their silent mime. The car enters the driveway, the sound a sigh of relief, for she is glad to have her husband return with the children. Three boys and two girls come in.

"Hello Mom!"

"Hello!"

"Hi, Brian," the youngest girl says, gamboling through the kitchen.

"Hi, Sara," the oldest boy says to his mother, imitating his brother Jake who also used her first name.

"How's the day been, Robert?" she responds.

He shrugs and opens the icebox; each child has looked in it and withdrawn something.

"Did Kilpatrick give you any trouble?" Mr. Grass asks, coming in with bags of groceries. She looks up and gives her husband a glance like someone in a procession gives to a spectator they recognize.

"Well, he won't be here much longer; next month he'll be gone; then I bet, the next time we see him, he'll have nothing but medals on, a Viet vet," Mr. Grass says, winking at Brian.

"There's a letter from Jake on the table," she says to Robert.

"Oh, wow, good; when is he going to send me a Gook ear? Boy, I've been waiting," Robert says.

"Robert, don't even say that in jest."

"Jest nothing; if he sent me enough of them I'd make a necklace," he says, skipping up to Brian, "wouldn't that be neat, Brian?" He laughs behind a cupped hand at his mother's consternation.

"Friends," he goes on, bowing to all corners of the kitchen and at his younger brothers who are laughing with him, "Friends, Romans, and Countrymen, lend me your *ears!* An *ear* a day keeps the Gooks away . . ."

He is president of his high school's freshman class.

"And further, there is nothing to fear, but EARS!"

"Robert!"

He leaves the kitchen with a graham cracker stuck halfway out of his mouth and with Jake's letter in his hand which he takes with him to read in the bathroom.

TWO

JAKE'S OPEN suitcase displays clothes he had packed away two years ago. Blue jeans, wool shirts, penny loafers. He puts on corduroy pants and takes out a clean pair of socks.

"Just a little ol' jungle rot; some soft mush feet, but they're beginning to firm back up now."

He slaps a foot and pulls up a sock.

"This place isn't that bad . . . for one person. Just sitting here is one beaucoup pleasure."

Jake pushes aside the window's shutters, looks down on the side street's parked cars, the Hudson River, the park's thin edge of green. They drink beer.

"The guy I was going to motorcycle across the country with got blown away a month before I left . . ."

His last letter from Vietnam had said he was planning to buy a motorcycle and "soak up some good ol' Americanis Ruralis et Urbanis." Brian asked him what happened. Blown away.

"So . . . after the airplane ride . . . we crossed the International Date Line, so I arrived the same day I left . . . big warehouse place, high dusty windows; signed out, couldn't even read my signature, my hand was shaking so. Still had my uniform on; couldn't wait to get out of it, but I just took the first plane out to Saint Louis. Got in about seven in the morning, called Lexa, and we spent the day in a motel room. She got sore. I never could come with whores in Nam; oh, maybe once or twice; they've got a thing in the villages, little shacks—dirt man, shit you couldn't believe, old rubbers stuck up on the wall, like pin-ups; they ask you: Want a hand job soldier, number one hand job. Very cheap. You lie down on a table and they go to work on you; first they get out this squeeze bottle, plastic-ketchup-piglet bottle from the PX, filled with some horrible kind of shit, some milky hand cream, jism juice concoction and smear that on your prick and they have at it. A lot of guys did that just because there's not much chance of catching anything; they were always asking me, 'Hey Doc, what can I do so I don't catch anything?' And I'd tell them, 'Just piss afterwards and that'll do it . . .' "

One of Jake's small brothers came home from a neighborhood park blowing up a condom, making a balloon of dirty glass. Brian started to take it from him, but Jake stopped him, saying, "Hey, we're not supposed to know what they are." Jake's mother, happening by a window, saw the scene and ran out the front door, snatching it from the young boy. She did not even look at Jake and Brian with a reprimand. Jake smiled smugly at Brian after the front door closed behind her.

Jake and Brian acquired that wholeness that comes with friendships made of opposites; they fell together, naturally contrasted; they were the long and short of it, Jake dark and Brian light. Their pairing completed a unit they were not fully aware of; these childhood matches happen often: They speak to difference, to that which we are not, an impulse to union.

At sixteen Jake was bolder with girls than Brian; once he had grabbed a girl's breasts, like he could palm a basketball, pressing them till the flesh under his fingernails turned blue. The three of them had been watching a colored TV in the bedroom of the girl's parents, the first they had seen. Brian had been surprised she didn't get angry, but just said in a low voice, "Oh, now you'll have to go to confession." Jake had laughed, punched Brian on the shoulder. Sixteen. A nature show was on the television, sooty elephants moving across green trees.

"No one's shooting at me now; you couldn't tell who you were going to get it from there. They're all Vietnamese. It's like giants in a dwarf world. I once came up behind the old man of the village, the most venerable man they had, and picked him up and swung him around like one of my little brothers; wow, did he get mad, hopping up and down, blabbering in Vietnamese. I just laughed; that's how it is; but it's the other Americans that get to you. Fucking shoot each other. We had this one top sergeant everyone hated, one bad motherfuck. Well, one day he goes off to take a shit—they cut drums in half and then when they get full, pour jet fuel in them and it burns away to nothing, jet fuel burns hot—a guy comes up behind the outhouse, lifts up the flap where you put in the barrel, pulls the pin on a grenade and lets the spoon fly. Waits, drops it in with a plop . . . runs like holy hell. The sergeant must have heard it drop cause he bursts out the door, struggling with his pants. Then it goes off. He got some fragments in his legs, but when he came back he was a bit more tame, wasn't such a bastard, because he knew it wouldn't take much for someone to blow him away for good.

"When you're out at some outpost you draw MP duty; everyone gets it, since it is such a bullshit thing to do. So I got it, went around with a black cat. The only time you know you're going to get any shit coming in, is when the twenty millimeter guns start. You can tell them a mile away, *birr-eep, bir-eep;* tear through anything. One night I'm inspecting a bunker and it's full of Souls, and they don't like me even looking in. They're all smoking dope—if you want a cigarette there, an American cigarette, you have to ask for a straight—I just nod to them and get the fuck out; but then the twenty millimeters start, and a siren comes on, and everybody is running around. But it's only some jackoff shooting at animals; all kinds of weird animals around the perimeter, and when somebody gets bored he just starts shooting them up. But then the brass comes and the guy goes into: 'They were coming, about thirty of them, but I chopped them up and they faded back . . .' So we're on alert for the rest of the night."

Jake leans out the open window, takes elaborate breaths.

"You never get use to the smell—man, I even dig this car exhaust. Shit, Brian, anyway you can get out, get out; that's all I got to say to you, except you probably won't go to Nam; well, I can't really say for sure. It's just so frustrating; following orders, from guys you wouldn't give the time of day to here, knowing they can really fuck you over if you don't do their shit.

"One night there was some incoming—some times you sleep on top of the bunkers because of the heat—you get just a little breeze there, so when the incoming started three guys were on top and two of them woke up, two white guys and the other a black dude who had been pretty drunk and was sleeping right through it; so the white guys just left him there, sleeping away as mortar rounds came in. It stopped and someone called for medics, so I go up with another and there he is, with half his head blown away. Big heavy blue-black cat. So we're putting him on a stretcher, I'm lifting him up by the shoulders and his head drops down and his brain falls out of his skull, or what's left of his skull; it falls out, *ka-plop;* I'm not going to pick it up. So we take him to the morgue tent and they zip him in a Jesus bag and truck him off to get a lube change.

Me and the other medic are scrubbing off the stretcher, you have to clean it well because blood rots canvas, and the chaplain comes up, a black one and is he pissed off, because he knows the guy was left there, so he says, real measured like, 'You clean it good boys,' and we go, 'Yes sir, yes sir.' "

2

"It's time to wake up, Jake," Mrs. Grass was calling, her voice drifting down the stairwell. Embers still glowed beneath the fireplace grate. The windows in the room were opening with light. Mrs. Grass had been down during the night, Brian knew, when he saw her trench coat over him. It had occurred three nights ago; then Jake and Lexa were asleep on the rug and Mrs. Grass had put a blanket over them. Brian, on the couch, received the trench coat. Lexa had flown back home yesterday to Saint Louis. The end of Jake's leave after basic training.

He came home with plaques and certificates: high scorer in physical combat training. Awarded to Pvt. Jacob Grass. They were thrown into a cardboard box and left on the third floor. Jake came quietly down to the bathroom on the second floor; he didn't want to awaken his brother Hank who shared the third floor with him but who wasn't going to the airport.

Ted Grass, the oldest brother, was an ensign on a

destroyer stationed in the Gulf of Tonkin. Brian had visited him in Newport, when Ted was finishing OCS. At a castle turned hotel they drank beer, watched the cardigan sweatered men and sun-darkened women play shuttlecock, while sailboats swirled in a bay like drowning moths.

"Tell him to join the navy," Brian had urged Ted, "write Jake; he's been staying in that windmill in Saint Louis, the plumbing broke down a month ago and they shit in paper bags and hurl it out the back door; Jake's let everything break down; he's just waiting to be drafted. Tell him to join the navy . . ."

Ted had picked up the heavy silverware setting and placed it piece by piece on the folded linen napkin, saying nothing, while a bar piano tinkled show tunes.

"Brian, are you up?" Mrs. Grass asked, looking into the living room.

"Hmmmm."

He followed her into the kitchen, rumpled tip to toe. Mrs. Grass moved about in the fluorescent tube's glow, Demeter's dim light, her hands held high in the readiness she assumed when fixing anything.

"You were doing your best to make this unsettled in my mind; but now it's all worked out so well, that Jake's to be a medic; it's just right for him," she said, making the same diagonal lines across the well-stepped kitchen, a lioness in her pen. She tried to subdue the echoes of early morning, but a few clattering calls rolled out.

"I've got to get everybody ready for school, or I'd go down too; but he's only going to Texas; it's not like he's really *leaving* . . ."

She stirs orange juice, thinking of the servings to the six younger children; their upcoming departures, across the yard, off to grammar school, the nuns ready, starched as the hour.

"There's so much to do; so much coming and going—I wish we'd get a letter from Ted; he keeps saying that there's nothing to write about floating in the ocean . . ."

She smiles; waves break on her jetty of recollections.

"Good morning," Mr. Grass says, coming into the kitchen, still buttoning his shirt.

"She didn't sleep at all last night," he says to Brian, "as nervous as if she was going to see Jesus ride through the shopping center today on a bicycle."

They share the first laughter of the morning.

"You fellows are no end of amusement to each other; one day zigzag lightning will get you both and I don't want to be around."

"Afraid it just might skip on over," Mr. Grass says, still chuckling.

"Do you have to start at six in the morning?" she says, going off to call up the stairs, softly: "Jake, it's time."

"When you come back from the airport I don't want you to cut your morning classes," she says to Brian. "Anytime you cut a class I know it means my housework is going to be interrupted."

Hearing footfalls she returns to the dining room. Jake stands dressed in his uniform in the hallway. The dark green square-cut coat fits his tall figure and hangs straight from wide shoulders. The creases in his pants are as sharp as Ted's officer's ceremonial saber. The brass insignia on his lapels are settled in baby-blue plastic edging.

"You're so pretty, Jake," his mother says, reaching up and smoothing his shoulder, trying to disguise the caress with practicality.

"Let's be off," his father says, "we have just enough time to make it to the airport."

"You're so pretty," his mother says once more.

"Yeah, I'm the nuts," Jake replies, grinning.

"You are pretty this morning, Jake," she says, calling after them as they climb into the car. She stares intently from the back porch until the automobile disappears up the street and she could see them no more.

"I WROTE you about the guy who jumped off the ship, didn't I?" Jake asks Brian. He had carried Jake's letters with him like a sacred pyx.

"He was hanging on the railing for about three seconds, hanging there like he was getting ready to do a regulation army chin-up, his back against the ship, and he just lets go. I pitied him then, but not so much now. I started to get the shakes with about a month left; it happens a lot to the short-timers. This buddy of mine, a huge black guy, sees me starting to shake, and I say, 'Man, I gotta hold on to something,' so he comes up and puts his arms around me, tries to hold me down . . .''

Jake drops cigarette ash out the window; Brian wonders what he would do if Jake began to shake now.

"I don't get them here much, but the first day with Lexa in the motel in Saint Louis they came on me when I was sitting in a chair and if she would have done anything but what she did I would have started to scream at her and would have walked out. I started to shake and without saying anything, or acting alarmed, she just came up and put her arms around me. Shit, Brian, it is fucking terrible; the worst thing—when I really felt it, was when I got off the plane.

"You hear stories. They tell you to watch yourself when you get back here in the States, because there's been cases of soldiers just getting back from Nam being shot when they get off the plane, usually by someone in a family of a boy who got killed there, some marine had just been shot by someone's mother a few days before I left. So you think about it a lot. So, I was watching out, and walking down a long narrow hallway and I heard some voices behind me, saying, I thought, 'There's one, let's get him,' and footsteps pick up and soon they are running up behind me, and I say, Oh, Jesus. So, I decide to wait till they get right behind me, then to swing around with my duffle bag, club the motherfuckers with it; it weighed over a hundred pounds. So, they're running and I'm waiting and they're right behind me, and I turn, the bag starting a real murderous arc—and it's just two kids, two teen-agers, a boy and girl, running to get somewhere and they stop and see me all wild-eyed and mouth twisted up and this bag ready to come down on them and I stop midway and they, in some sort of horror at this becrazed soldier ready to bust their pumpkin heads, leap back against the wall and just quiver there.

"I throw the bag down and sit on it, mumbling to them; and they just run away from me. I sat there on the bag and cried. I don't know what for; self-pity, me, them, fucking Vietnamese. I just cried and began to shake . . ."

They had talked so often in their nonage; long monologues of aspiration, sitting in the dark on a porch, during the mild midwestern nights, dreaming together. Jake looks at Brian, makes a gesture of finality, flinging his hand as if tossing pebbles into a still pond, shattering the reflected image.

"My entrance back into the good ol' U.S.A. I guess it was then I decided just to hotfoot it back to Saint Louis, to get hold of Lexa, to get back, to find a little continuity. Man, there was a movie on the jet that took us away from Nam. *War Wagon.* I couldn't believe it. But Saint Louis, warm, fragrant, familiar Saint Louis county . . . and Lexa.

"Later, that day, I was asking her half-jokingly if she had been faithful and all that; she confessed that she had gone out with one boy and had made out a little. I got mad; I yelled and threatened to leave her . . ."

"You can't be serious, Jake, one episode," Brian said.

"No sir, Brian, the ol' double standard; anyway, she cried and we made up and I forgave her, but she wants to get married and I don't know what the fuck I want to do. Doing this hardware gig with my old man; I know nothing now. Right. Wrong. Bullshit—everything is very simple: I'm alive. You do what you do to stay that way. Explain, Brian, what should I do?

"I started school, GI Bill and all that, and everyone in the class was a kid; I came into a social science class the first day—there was a young woman teaching it. I was late and opened the door and she was standing right next to it, so I knocked her down coming in; so I helped her get up and then I dropped my stack of IBM cards on the floor, so I stooped down for that and the whole class was watching and she red-faced at having been knocked over, so I walked back to the only empty desk in the back and dropped my books and bending over to pick them up I cut the biggest . . . loudest . . . fart and everyone starts to laugh . . ."

Jungle gas spread over Social Science 101; Nam smell, contraband fart smuggled into the States.

"Then she made me come up to the front of the class and *apologize* for cutting a fart . . ."

Apologize for the Vietnam fart gas brain rot smell; sorry ma'am, guts aren't emptied of rice and bananas and C rations and sirloin death stench; sorry.

"So, I quit at the end of the first week; it just wouldn't

work out; not right now anyway; maybe in a year. Now I sell pliers and staples. The motto of our company, painted on a sign atop the factory is: 'You can't live life without the staples.'"

THREE

"You boys going home now?"

Her voice passes out from under a two-foot silver wig. She stands under a darkened Broadway movie marquee, across from a newsstand kiosk. Brian and Jake look back at her.

"Hey, should we?"

"Buy? Are you kidding?"

Brian tried to show Jake the city available to him. The streets, the bars; a countryboy's debauch. The tall black woman goes back into the shadows, backwards, a midnight glockenspiel.

"Both of us?"

"I don't have any cash left . . ."

"You get used to fucking and it doesn't really matter a whole hell of a lot with whom . . ."

"Jake, I don't care . . ."

They walk on, through the Upper Broadway crowd, jostling the night's sidewalk phantasmagoria.

The white eagle at the street's end hovers in its spotlight. Bright facets of the buildings on the New Jersey palisade fling reflections on the Hudson's thick undulating side. The hall of the brownstone, plumbing drool down the dull walls, carpet is shredding on the steps, the banisters are out of plumb and the bare bulb on the second floor landing is a skull unfleshed. They go into the room, city foxhole, New York bunker.

"Let's go back and get her . . ."

"That chick looked like a chrome dildo . . ."

"It wasn't till I got in the army that I realized I had a cock; before, all that dry-fucking," Jake says, with an expression of distaste, "certified-approved-Roman-Catholic-finger-fucking . . ."

Double-dating to drive-in movies: feeling a zipper, brassy teeth, a callus on the abdomen. Fogged-over windows, speakers hung from them, movie dialogue swelling the darkness. Midwestern voodoo masks, those drive-in car speakers. Straps, hooks, the girl's underwear feeling like warmed cellophane, her moisture dampening the thin fabric like wind through a screen.

Jake, looking back over the front seat, laughing, throwing popcorn down on Brian and his date. *How far did you get?* Some inner landscape; I was repulsed at the great divide. *The grape divide?* Laughter. Later, when they

went to Winstead's for Cokes and onion rings they all
noticed stuck onto the letter of Jake's high school ring, a
coiling pubic hair.

"Yeah, I fucked some chicks, especially some terrible
ones in Texas, that I wouldn't care to see again, lest I'm
haunted for good . . . why don't we go back and
get . . ."

"It's after three, the Howard Johnson's at nine tomorrow; wake me up, I'll go down with you . . ."

"A buddy of mine who got out three months ago,
named Dutch, lives with his parents in Queens. I have his
phone number; Dutch is too much; we were out on
perimeter once and had to build bunkers; everybody took
it real serious for a while, but we just wanted to get the
fuck finished; we put the sandbags anywhere—Man, I hate
sandbags—and then we put poles across the top, then
stretched tents, ponchoes, plastic bags from mortar rounds,
anything that looked waterproof over them, then more
sandbags. It rains like hell, most of them collapsed, water
runs through in streams. Ours didn't fall down, but it
leaked; we got soaked. So, Dutch says he's not going to get
wet the next night, so he blows up his air mattress, covers
himself with his poncho and goes off to sleep. I'm next to
him and two other guys are next to me. Around midnight
it starts raining again . . . and hard. Dutch has kicked off
his poncho since it's hot and then . . ."

Jake starts laughing, beating his legs against the bed like
a novice swimmer. Brian starts to laugh.

"So . . . Dutch . . . is on his air mattress . . . and the water starts coming through . . . and he floats . . . *floats* . . . out the bunker and on down the path . . . he wakes up in the morning with a water buffalo chewing by his ear . . ."

Tears run out of their eyes; Jake gasps for breath.

"Sheee-it. He's a little shorter than you; never saw a guy quite like that for swearing . . ."

"ARE YOU sure you don't want to come?"

"No, I can't; I've got to go on up to class . . ."

Jake wanted Brian to go with him to Queens and see Dutch's home movies of the war.

Brian, it is a pretty sight to watch those spinning silver canisters of napalm come right down on top of where all the fire has been coming from. . . .

Brian, on the boat trip over, about a day after the kid jumped, the air turned really foul, and something floated into view, like a huge marshmallow, about as big as this room; turned out to be whale blubber. There were about thirty or forty sharks around its edge, snapping at it, eating, turning over and swallowing; it floated along side us for about a half an hour. . . .

Brian, I'm really not sure I killed anyone; once there were two old men in a rice paddy and we were on patrol, *Search and Avoid,* and when they saw us they dropped their hoes and ran off so the lieutenant ordered us to fire on them; I had one in my sights, but raised above him and fired. If they knew I did something like that I could have been court-martialed. . . .

Dutch had come yesterday, wearing civilian clothes with the unnatural fit of a released convict's free suit. Working for the phone company. Jake and he quickly recounted the few months they had been separated. Dutch asked about Lexa; Jake wondered if Dutch had found a girl. Dutch demurred, living with his parents; there isn't much out in Queens, hardly ever comes into Manhattan, the City.

"Did they give you a parade when you got home?" he asked Jake, knowing the answer would be the same, for as they shared the same life in Vietnam, their reception was the same when they returned.

"Oh, sure, man," Jake had said, laughing, "banners and streamers. We come back to the States, left off at the border, and we infiltrate back to our hometowns."

"They're paying him to go to school," Jake said, pointing to Brian. Dutch turned to look at him as if he was lifting his head from off a sickbed.

So you're selling hardware now?

How's the phone company?

"Dutch isn't very entertaining, but he's a nice guy," Jake had said. They went drinking in Village bars. Dutch had to leave early because it was a long drive back to Queens and work began at eight. The sentries of responsibility were posted around his days.

Dutch honks his car's horn below in the street.

"Sure you don't want to go?"

"I can't Jake; I have two classes."

What am I to do? Jake had asked Brian. I've taken this job, Lexa wants to get married and I don't know what the fuck is happening. Most times I just want to be alone. Stay in New York? Get a job here? I hate this city. Any suggestions, Brian? All the Vietnams in the world ain't going to get me into an Ivy League university. . . .

They seemed to talk to each other through the visitor's wire mesh of a penitentiary. Penitent century. For the last three days Jake bade Brian put his fingers in his wounds.

Jake's badge from the manufacturer's convention sat on the bureau. A white card in a plastic casing.

JAKE GRASS
Salesman
GLAD TO MEET YOU!

Yesterday they arrived at the Howard Johnson's and Mr. Grass greeted them and said to Jake: "Comb your hair."

You might have been fucking over the Viet Cong four weeks ago but this is the lobby of the Howard Johnson's and the Coliseum awaits.

Businessmen gladiators wander through, briefcase

shields at their sides, newspaper cudgels under their arms. Eighth Avenue lions, the stalls of the hardware show, the slave market displays, lawnmowers over paper grave grass. Aisles of implements, pencils score the orders, carbon-paper stains on their fingers, black bile, Babel language, liquor bottles uprighted and spouted like cow udders. WELCOME HARDWARE MEN. Hard used, hard wear men. Jake is introduced as a Vietnam veteran, a recent warrior. Can't hurt sales. Cancer scales.

JAKE BAFFLES the roar of the city. His shell of stories held to Brian's ear leaves New York's clamor just an ocean's soft tidal lapping.

"Lexa wants me to come back right away; she's having some sort of family crisis. Dad's leaving today; I guess I'll go back; no use staying on here. There's a three o'clock train; I'm supposed to meet him."

Jake dresses in a new suit, bought with his service savings bonds.

"I'll enjoy the ride back, some nice country we cross . . ."

Brian envies his unsteady signature on his release papers. Release. Jake is free; *free*. Of the men in his platoon, eight left, he untouched. What angles around him in the furnace? Mrs. Grass's prayers answered; no other explanation would be as suitable to her.

"Do you ever mention the bad shit to your parents?"

"No; why should I?"

Why should he? They needn't be shaken; the floats of their temperment would adjust to it.

"Why should I tell them I fell down one day; slipped on a piece of someone like a banana peel . . ."

Night storms could rend the sky, but like a statue in a courtyard Mrs. Grass's features would return unforeboding on the morrow. I have lost one son and am prepared to lose another.

They pull their collars tight against a bitter wind and hail a cab on West End Avenue.

"Well, Brian, I'm leaving you to New York and the winter . . ."

Jake is so tall that he sits uncomfortably in the cab like an unfolded multipurpose knife. Where would you like to eat? What kind of food would you like? Brian had asked the first night.

"Any kind," Jake had answered, "as long as it's American."

"THE TRAIN's been delayed," Mr. Grass said, "something about a bridge not going down."

Jake puts his foot up on his suitcase.

"Don't do that, Jake, think of the dirt you've stepped on . . ."

Mr. Grass rubs the spot with tissue, like a nurse

preparing a patient for an injection. He makes an unpleasant, grim face.

"Brian, don't you find you have to wash your hair more often?" he says, jokingly.

"Really, this is the dirtiest city in the world. Three and a half days is too long to remain . . ."

Waiting sours the minutes. It is announced that trains would leave from a station in New Jersey. The milling thickens. It is recommended that the travelers take bus transportation to New Jersey. The crowd diminishes; a few commuters remain despondent on the benches. The electric sound of calculation rises above the muttering discontent. Frustrated. It adds up to nothing. Announcement boards show ANNULLED after each trains' name.

Jake, his father, and Brian leave the station. Mr. Grass had sought out directions. They were to go to Macy's, to Herald Square, and they would find a PATH train to New Jersey.

Brian carries one of Mr. Grass's bags; he would not allow him to take both. Jake manages his two; they stop often to rest, Mr. Grass daubs his brow with a handkerchief, the bad air worries his expression. The buildings have flushed their occupants onto the streets; they move with the concerted haste of a population fleeing an imperiled city. The luggage makes sliding through the crowd difficult. Next to his son and under the day's stress Mr. Grass assumes a frailty Brian had never before seen.

A news vendor shouts, folds a paper, and snaps it under men's arms that are not free: a nightly inoculation. Stone buildings dull in the sapped light. New York refugees making ready for the night's occupation.

Reaching Herald Square they are caught in a riptide rush. Stairs leading down to the PATH trains are flooded with people; the lines at the turnstiles are lengthy and slow. Mr. Grass says he cannot stand to wait in those lines. His face is gray with fluorescent waiting-room fatigue.

They go back up the steps, fighting the white water advance of those coming down. The smell of Macy's candy counter cloys the air, sickly mixed with cosmetics. They are expelled onto the street, facing Herald Square. There, by the subway entrance, a huge figure sits on a brass stanchion. A shoebox in her lap, a cotton dress. Her face a seizure of screams, purple gums meshed with mucous. Her visage is a plea for she is silently begging, sitting there, half-woman, half-stone. A few coins are in her box.

Mr. Grass notices her and quickly looks away, shaking his head, as if all the city's diseases were contained in the woman.

Her legs are swollen the size of telephone poles. Her feet are encased in something, but not shoes. Fluids from many smiling sores run down her legs.

"Syphilis," Jake says, observing.

. . . the air turned really foul, something floated into view, like a huge marshmallow and there were about thirty or forty sharks around its edge, snapping at it, eating, turning over and swallowing . . .

A woman on a brass hydrant in front of Macy's. Running sores. Sharks' smiles.

Mr. Grass spies an empty cab in traffic, with *New Jersey Cab Co.* painted on its side. He steps off the curb and stops it. Jake and Brian stand silently, the city having made mutes of them.

"Will you take us to New Jersey?" Mr. Grass asks the driver. He nods yes.

. . . his brain falls out of his skull, *ka-plop* . . .

Mr. Grass motions to Jake and the bags are shoved into the cab. Brian shakes Mr. Grass's hand.

"Give my love to them all back home . . ."

"Thank you, Brian, for the help with the bags . . ."

. . . starting a murderous arc and it's just two kids, they stop and see me all wild-eyed and mouth twisted up and this bag ready to come down on them, ready to bust their pumpkin heads . . .

"Jake, it was great seeing you . . ."

Jake's arm waves back at Brian; the cab is taken up, then lost in the congealing traffic.

Brian turns to leave. The brass hydrant is vacant; two python heads linked by chain. Down the emptying street Brian follows the glistening trail of her departure.

FOUR

THE CAMPUS was still held in aftermath's unnatural calm. A few students lingered on the grounds; it was avoided, a sacred grove that had been profaned, which had lost its magic with the first entrance of the helmeted police. The brick walks, fountains, stone benches, grottoed statuary, the small lawns in the shadows of the buildings, shaded with trees, were laced with the eerie quiet of a well-preserved battlefield. Its atmosphere; at most, fear.

Lofty, low-rising steps that humbled the climber with the necessity of taking halting half-steps, led to the pantheon, Low Library. These elevations, cement and marble representations of hierarchy, advancement, formed an uncurving amphitheater. These steps are templar, the bases of public monuments, found fronting government buildings, are shrined in our dreams. Climb, succeed, elevate yourself, conquer.

The days of registration a handful of young people wore

red armbands, talked of strikes, occupation of buildings, shutting the university down. They were *rara avis* and soon were not seen; they disappeared all at once like the dark waves of migratory birds.

HOMER HERODOTUS SOPHOCLES PLATO ARISTOTLE DEMOSTHENES CICERO VERGIL Brian reads from the arras of Butler Library. When he first stepped on the university's college walk he had the feelings immigrants are said to have when they first sight the Statue of Liberty. In the Midwest, the East was thought of by Brian as being no less mysterious than Marco Polo's. He registered at the university as if he was checking into a Grand Hotel. He expected to be leaving at any time.

Workmen sandblasted the street-side walls, erasing the initials and slogans of last spring's uprising. But the pigment had gone deep into the porous stone and even after the fierce embrasure their shadows remained, ghostly transparent images, secret writing: BRING THE WAR HOME.

AN ELEVATOR leaps ten floors at a time. Launch pad equivalents; every cleric an astronaut ascending to his capsule. Lights flash, numbers glow and dim, technology's display for each of its citizens. Federal Building: Selective Service Headquarters. Women at desks, filicide rooms, drudge Medeas. Coffee break paper cups are marked with the stains of passing time. Bomb shelter serenity prevails.

No decorations on gray walls, except for a glass-framed needlepoint of the selective service seal. A comorant with lightning bolt spears in its claws. On a row of filing cabinets a cardboard cut-out figure, a soldier leaping some unseen obstacle, a rifle held diagonally across his chest.

"Can I help you?"

"I want to transfer my induction order . . ."

Name, address, age, reason for transfer, occupation. She puts down *student*. She types at a hulking electric machine with one finger.

"Is there someone I can see to answer a few questions? My semester ends in January, so I was wondering if there was any chance of getting my induction postponed a month?"

"Just a moment; Maria," she calls to an older woman; they consult.

"Perhaps Major Sanjuaniwojimo can talk to you," she says, and puts a call through.

"Yes; you can go back; his name is on the door."

A major, Brian thinks, I'm going to talk to a major.

No uniform, a blue business suit; about forty-five.

"Yes, what is it you want?"

Brian repeats his request.

"Just a minute . . ." He dials. "I've got Kilpatrick in here; he just transferred his induction order; is there any way the paper work on that can be delayed till January? Yes. I see. I wouldn't want to break the rules. Yes. Thank you.

"There's more than one way to skin a cat," he says, hanging up. "A directive has been issued that allows graduate students to finish the semester they are in, if they are drafted during that time; I don't know how things are west of the Mississippi, but I imagine it is the same. I was just trying to avoid all the unnecessary paperwork. Now, you write your draft board and request a postponement till the end of the semester, which they probably will grant; then they will send us an order to cancel your induction and they will draft you again, probably for February, then you'll come back here, I suppose, and transfer. We could have probably saved all that paper work if you would have talked to me first; we could have just held things up till January."

The major turns in his swivel chair, looks steadily out a window, studies the river, smoking industrial stacks, street runes through the irregular granite surface below.

"So, we'll see you then . . ."

"Thank you," Brian says, raising his hand, waving good-bye, which, as he shuts the door, he realizes was an embryonic salute.

He leaves as if he is truly escaping. A cripple who dreams he can walk. He has till March if it works out, he figures, marveling at the dice-throw of circumstance. March. Four months. March. He pantomimes a goosestep, goes out the building's high glass doors and is received by the streets, the subway, the cold.

ANY NEW sight is a counterfeit event and for weeks Brian's solitude, the fact that he is alone, is not obvious; he is then shocked by the suddenness with which it fells him. The reasons he tells himself for his being alone seem sufficient for a single instance, but they are unsatisfactory when a number of them are put together.

He eats by himself in large cafeterias. There, unattached persons place themselves the farthest space from one another until they are all gravely equidistant.

At night Brian stands at his window and sees a television screen in the building across the street; another in an apartment a floor beneath. They show the same program.

The time thus diminished, and as a set of lenses which by adjustment brings far-off objects into focus, Brian is forced to define the limits of his choices. You go into prison as a witness; or you go because there is nothing else you can do. Are there years to discard? he wonders. Both the thoroughly evil and thoroughly good made him uneasy.

Some men are virtuous only because they haven't the strength to implement their faults. Brian realizes he is too unsure of himself to lie; Jake was a marvelous liar.

Jake and Lexa were to marry; they wanted Brian to return to the Midwest for the wedding. Brian hadn't the money and did not want to leave with the draft unresolved.

A saucer is littered with single burnt-out matches. How many individual times have I lit the gas burner? Brian wonders, looking at the matches which lie in rows like primitive counting scratchmarks. A crescent of grease wanes in a pan. Cockroaches have nested behind the burlap he had put up on the walls of the alcove above the sink and refrigerator; their legs and feelers stick out through the coarse weaving. The icebox latch had broken and Brian put a chair up against its door. The sink is shallow, filled with dishes, stuck with the sauce of canned ravioli dinners.

Before he sleeps, Brian stares forlornly at the sperm in the toilet bowl. It resembles drowned earth worms that are found in pools of standing water left after a night's rain. He flushes it down.

THE HALL's inner door bangs behind Brian.

"O.K. buddy. . . ."

Three black boys running, knives out; they wave them over their heads like Independence Day sparklers.

On the landing Brian is cornered. A thick bowie knife creases his throat. A long switchblade pricks his side. The third gesticulates with a small Boy Scout knife, outside the pack Brian and the other two form; he runs around trying to find an entrance in. Some children's game. Brian has one hand in his pocket, the other holds the damp weight of the Sunday *New York Times*. Shit, he thinks, I didn't even realize they were behind me. The Boy Scout knife gets his wallet; the only Sunday he has had more than a dollar left in it. Nine. Scraps of identification fall out, driver's license from Missouri, a university ID, draft card, shreds of addresses, telephone numbers, a laundry ticket.

They are eighteen or nineteen, thick with winter clothes. The bowie knife wears black Converse tennis shoes. Will they cut me? Brian makes an instant human tabulation, for if he decides they will he must fight. No. They fill up the landing; the light down in the hall glows like a cave's hidden lake. A hand reaches in his pocket to get coins.

"Hey man, leave me some change . . ."

"Tyrone, leave him his change . . ."

The Boy Scout knife picks up the spill from the wallet, replaces it, a wild civility.

"Tyrone, all of it . . ."

"What is this shit calling me by my name motherfuck, keep names out of it," Tyrone spits out, more hurt by the dressing down than the lapse of security. He bends his head back away from Brian, turning the blade to its wide flat side on Brian's neck. It is as cold as a frosted pane of glass. The other had not moved the switchblade poking his side, long as a knitting needle. Contact, robbery intimacy; the scout knife takes the wallet, holds it in front of Brian, like a stick to a dog, and throws it up the rest of the flight of stairs to the second floor. They push off him like sprinters from starting blocks. Tyrone gives a fist salute. Gone. The hall is empty; Brian climbs the rest of the way to his room.

FIVE

A PHONE booth filled with snow. The accordion door is wedged open. Brian dials. A mutual aquaintance had given him her number. Blue, electrical sounds; he stamps his cold feet, his cowboy boots leak through their soles. A buzzing sound.

She's there anyway, Brian thinks. Tonight I thought I'd make certain of all the slights I've received; it was a New Year's resolution . . . something to tell her.

I'll drop you a card when to come over, she had said, the first time he had called, since you haven't a phone . . . that must make you feel important, being so hard to reach. . . .

No card. He had expected it the following week, over a month ago. He had pictured something delicate, a gracious script. She's home anyway, he thinks, dialing again.

"WHEN DO you want to see me?"

"Now."

When do you want to see me?

Now. *Now.* A number five bus, sun cracking open on the windows like an egg. The passenger's long roots of odors from sitting, the hoarse distribution of the gears, the sounds levitate. Audrey is a silver hoop for Brian that he passes around the suspended body of sensation. Reaching her last night, she had said: "Bring your hiking shoes . . ." Five flights up an East Side walk-up; stairs either increase dejection or expectation. He left at four in the morning, saying to himself, if I never see her again I still have had seven hours; and now: "When do you want to see me?"

"Now, I've thought of you most of the day . . ."

The bus goes down a bad cut of Broadway. Brian is tolerant; he makes excuses; he enjoys the ride.

"I'm glad to see you; you're the mooring to my sanity, things are out of hand . . ."

Brian starts to speak; she stops him.

"We are not alone . . ."

He hadn't noticed. A woman Audrey's age sits on the rug, smoking. They are introduced. She offers Brian the marijuana. Breaking bread; new oral customs.

"No thanks; I'm not an enthusiast . . ."

The woman, Rhea, heavy, a Jewess given to lavender, shrugs, "No big deal . . ."

Audrey talks softly over the phone, agrees to something.

"Vanessa's taken acid for the first time with Link; he just returned from the Coast. This morning I didn't get to work; an hour after you left I got a call." (Did she think it from me? Brian asks himself.) "And it's a friend of a friend—this seems to be the week for them—who's in town waiting to leave for London. So he arrives. I haven't had any sleep, then Vanessa finally decides to go on this trip with Link and she wants me along, either on the trip or as a chaperone; so the four of us spent the day in Central Park; London-bound is at a movie now—doesn't talk much . . ."

She prepares dinner, cutting and paring, a palm full of greens.

"When you called a month ago I was going to arrange a party, but I lost your address. It's extraordinary that you don't have a phone . . ."

How many evenings, weeks, months without speaking to a young woman, Brian thinks; and here, sitting around a table, surrounded, making them laugh. He tries to appear that this is his natural state. He wonders how long it will take till the surprise is removed from his face that remains from his first sight of her.

"I don't look like a Miss Connecticut, do I? Someone told me that earlier in the week . . ."

The phone rings. "Vanessa wants me to come upstairs; will you excuse me for a moment?"

"Flo Nightingale of the drug culture," Rhea says to her departing back.

Link enters, an androgynous Chinese. Bloused, zipperless Mexican peasant pants, a sash, bare feet, heavy, round-rimmed black glasses. Vanessa follows, long red hair, rococo waves, shirt unbuttoned, pastel jeans, an English accent. Link, in a matter of minutes, seems to be many entities to her—man servant, lover, brother, friend, business associate. They are kept distinct with a gesture, inflection, if not hers, his.

"I brought back some great Dallas purple . . ."

A photographer; Vanessa operates a boutique in the basement of the building.

Audrey sits by Brian. The out-of-town guest returns from the movie; tall, bushy hair, his body bowed by his height. Crashing across the country; awaiting a charter flight to London. They talk; each speaker embellishes what is said before, an echo is achieved, the words repeating themselves, off the encroaching walls, comforting to them, soporific. The movement is very slow, drug discourse, reiterated, redundant agreement.

"We went up to a mounted policeman who didn't have his horse in Central Park and we asked him why. He was obviously a mounted policeman without a mount; you could feel the emptiness between his legs; so we asked him and he said it was too cold for the horse and we sympathized with him for about five minutes . . ."

"A mounted policeman without a mount . . . weird . . ."

"In Dallas a group of us went to the airport and lay down at the end of the runway and then let the jets take off over us. The noise, the vibrations, like the end of the world: the heat, the vibrations, the noise . . ."

"Why is he sitting there? Whoever sits next to him starts to talk; I want to talk; come sit next to me, catalyst . . ."

Audrey was a woman of whom there are likenesses, but not duplicates. They are all as appealing from a distance. They are not wizened from being weaned off poverty; at least one comfortable generation precedes them. She was a woman whose looks are completed early. Set at twenty for two decades. She would age like a painting.

"But," Rhea says to Vanessa, "you can do nothing better than anyone."

"Vanessa," Audrey adds, "you're too involved in all that faggot frippery . . ."

Brian, as outsider, can only recognize the thrusts at each other; the glinting blade that picks up the least of the light. They have histories behind them; years of observed intimacy. They are a tribe Brian has only just discovered.

Accusations, recollections of weaknesses, strands of the past used as a cat-o'-nine-tails on each other's backs. The three women scratch at the grounds of their friendship like hens for seed. Link grins. The guest from the movie closes his eyes, folds his hands on his lap like an ant hill.

"I feel like going home," Audrey says.

"You are home," Link replies.

"I know; that's the trouble . . ."

The apartment assumes an overfull lifeboat's silence; who is the dead weight? The tall guest who has been recumbent throughout rises up, uncoils like a chimney's first smoke, and says, "I'm going to call a hotel."

Rhea begins to oversee him. Vanessa and Link rise up and wander down the hall, hand in hand, as if it were a forest's edge; lost in the shadows they return to Vanessa's apartment, two flights up.

"George can stay at my place tonight," Rhea announces. Off to London.

Brian has been with Audrey a dozen hours and he thinks himself an archaeologist with her past. And this room, a tomb sealed for a thousand years because all its artifacts tell a history he has never known.

He feels an odd familiarity with Audrey, if not with her friends. It is that which two people in a waiting room share, one having returned and the other ready to start out.

NOISE IS the hourglass of passing time in a city and now

even Fifty-eighth Street is quiet. Brian saw Audrey was upset; those silent accumulations you can never gauge—stalagmites building up in entranceless caves. Last night she seemed to be the years older that she is; even the voice had been firmer: a taut line of implied distance. But now she is agitated and he tries to comfort her, having seen it take place, a witness who can testify in your behalf. Where Vanessa had baited her, Rhea's nettles.

She begins to cry, placing her hands on her eyes and drawing down her lids as an attendant does to a corpse. And though he does not comprehend the reasons for her small sobs he tries to quiet her; no woman will weep in front of you unless she feels some safety.

He caresses the side of her head and she reaches up and brings him down on her. She holds him tightly; he cannot move without forcing so there he remains, while her tears abate, held to her chest, like something she clings to that was almost snatched away. He cannot believe she clings to him.

Half the world's embraces are awkward and Brian with difficulty works his arms around her. He imagines her thinking, now that she is still, "What am I going to do with him?" He turns his head to kiss her neck and she manages to prevent it. He really doesn't care; being used to nothing, this, like a child with a nickel, is a fortune. He persists. He feels her throat's hollowness, her diminutive scimitar eyelashes, the thin membrane of flesh over her eye, like ignorance over an idea.

"I don't want to make love tonight . . . that bedroom is haunted."

The room regains its shape; Brian realizes it has begun to rain.

"I want to get to know you; look at you. I want some foundation . . ."

He senses in what she says some kind of warning; like a European road sign, recognizable, but not familiar. She leans her head back, arches her throat, Artemis's bow. Her blouse has three buttons near the neck; he undoes them and strokes the top of her breasts. She keeps her head bent back, her long blonde hair falls straight down, a golden plumb line. "Don't do that," Brian says, lifting her head, thinking her neck must be stiff, "It'll be sore."

"You must have thought I was asleep," she says and goes down the hall to the bathroom.

He thinks dejectedly of the way back to his room in the rain.

Audrey walks soundlessly into the room. Going from zero to one hundred with no numbers in between, he thinks, someone to talk to, don't push it.

"I'll be off," he says, thinking himself gallant.

"You don't have to go . . ."

He sees she has taken her nylons off.

She goes into her bedroom; Brian trails behind her like the gulls which follow a vessel.

A white bulb the size of a crystal ball is suspended over the bed. She sits and reaches her hand back behind her as if she is going to pull an arrow out of a quiver and off comes her blouse.

Brian fumbles with his boots, staring at her. She unhooks her brassiere and as she does her smile sets into one of whimsical resignation. He lets that pass. She has the unsuckled breasts of a young girl. As her hand begins to unclasp her skirt she shuts off the light. Afterglow capers before his wide eyes. Where are you? Why doesn't the moon shine through the airshaft? Then he finds her in his arms.

In the darkness Audrey has changed substance and now is all veins, wet chambers of chemical exchange, spongy, recuperative tissue. Women trail their hands in water when boating for it is such a similar element; they recognize its division and rejoining. Her locks give way. Entering her, each inch an epoch of desire.

"There, doesn't that feel good?" she says.

Pedestaled by infrequency, after so many nights of longing, it seems worth it to Brian, for once in her, in her arms, where else could he have been?

"Just stay right there . . ."

She entwines a leg around his, tightening herself. In the dark, sensation gathers into image, hovers suspended, coalesces into a kernel, thoughts that are complete but only last an instant; they remain a thing you apprehend but do not need to name. As a tossed stone sets off concentric rings in water her muscles begin to contract and expand.

Swallowing, Brian thinks.

The thinnest stain of light seeps into the room, chalks Audrey's face. A Japanese dancer in heavy powder. They invert; she kneels above him then slowly sinks down. The sound of two cupped hands squeezing paste. Audrey bends down to his mouth, kissing, a bird forcing food down a fledgling's throat. Her pelvis begins to jerk.

"Shit . . ."

She grabs onto his shoulders, till the spasm, like a train through a small town, passes.

"Shit . . . shit . . . shit."

The word shakes out of her mouth like pennies from a china bank.

And, as if she is a machine with the finest tolerances, she begins to shake, bouncing off her pinions, breaking apart since everything has fallen out of balance. Brian ludicrously thinks of his family's washing machine jumping in the basement. She throws herself down on him, collapses, liquids running out of them both. For a time they hold onto each other tightly, as if they are trying to shield each other from an impending explosion.

Brian slips out of her with the smoothness of a lock falling open when you reach the last number of a combination. Audrey sighs excrementally.

Thin bamboo curtains over the living room's window are blue cataracts of light. They shift about on the bed, arranging themselves.

"I've found this way works best," she says.

Brian has one hand on a breast, the other brushing her belly with his fingertips.

"I'll never be able to sleep after that," she says, pushing up on one arm like a new foal trying to stand, "I need a shot of heroin."

She reaches up to a shelf above the bed and glass jars clink.

"Heroin," he says, squinting seriously, "Just what-the-fuck . . ."

Audrey sits holding a small cylinder in front of her eyes as if she is reading a centigrade table. The sound of compressed air leaking.

"Oh, be serious; it isn't heroin; I have some light type of asthma; I was just kidding. I wouldn't be able to sleep through the night . . ."

"You and your heroin . . ."

Her shoulder goes up and down in silent laughter.

Lying along her back, like an outlaw hiding behind low boulders, he stares out into the room, awaiting dawn, for the bulky shapes in the room to dry out in the day's sun. He is amazed; he doesn't know what to think. But nothing much matters to him, wrapped around her, one of Audrey's breasts in his hand. He feels her heart beating. The steady beat of her heart drops into the palm of his hand like small silver coins.

SIX

COOING. TRILLING. Gurgling. Small throats vibrating. Kissing. A gourd dips in a stream. Somnambulant embraces. Arms in heavy water. Quay lips.

"Good morning. Tired still?"

Pigeons coo in the airshaft. The phone rings; Audrey laughs into the receiver. Brian suddenly feels like a successful imposter; who was it that he was supposed to be?

"Yes, he's still here," she says, smiling at him.

"Why do I sound happy? Because I am happy . . ."

Her bathroom is full of little things. Brian returns, conscious of his nakedness. She is still on the phone.

"Buy-I."

A silence; when do those spaces become treacherous?

"You are quiet in the morning; at night I can't shut you up."

"A woman should make a man speechless," he says, kidding.

She laughs. "Going to fix you breakfast." She stands up abruptly; his stomach tightens at the sight. The doorbell rings; she puts on a robe, quilted, Chinese. It sounds to him like Vanessa. A muted clatter comes from the kitchen.

"Hey, wake up; no fair going back to sleep; I have to go to work."

She holds a tray; halved grapefruit, vapor lifts off the surface of the tea. They talk; their words stoop over and pick up the things they had left scattered on the floor from last night. Space-flight time, Brian thinks, thirty-six hours into Audrey's life.

"I've got to be going," she says.

Water runs; pigeons coo; he drinks from his cup. He retrieves his sloughed underwear, pulls on his pants, sits on the edge of the bed; tired? Stunned?

"Oh!" Audrey stands in the doorway, wrapped in a pink towel.

She sits by him, smelling of soap, damp strands of hair touch his shoulder; their chill stings him. His hand starts to shake excitedly, resting lightly on her back. The towel loses its hold and falls across her lap. "I've got to go," she says, jumping up. "I'm an hour late already."

She can't know that she is the first woman Brian has been able to leisurely examine; furtiveness had shielded the others. She opens a small drawer, takes out tights, sets it, a light brown tuft, on the chest of drawers and from a row of bottles chooses some cream and rubs it on her legs, quickly, a frequent gesture. Brian knows he will be jealous of her habits, because they were formed without him. Pubic hair shows through her tights, a black pupil in a brown iris, a dog's eye.

"You should see the expression on your face," she says to him and then she begins to blush.

"You are quiet," she says, "I'm at my best right when I wake up, it's metabolism . . ."

She has her address book open.

"Shall I put you in? In pencil? I still don't know what to call you. Oh, well; here're the keys; just leave them in the mail box. Call me."

He showers surrounded by her odors. He looks at the empty bed, memory already reassembling like a lizard regrowing its tail. He leaves a note: THE PLACE IS YOURS AGAIN; MY WISH TOO, TO BE YOURS AGAIN.

The sharp winter sunlight cleaves Fifty-eighth Street. It parts before Brian, triumphantly, like the Red Sea.

SEVEN

THE ANTEROOM'S tabletops are covered with pamphlets. Testimonials of pacifism, Quaker tracts; it is as if the fervor of belief cannot sustain more than their dozen pages. Ceremonies, too, can only be so long; it is only during a speech of complaint that no one is at a loss for words. An old woman in a modest gray gown tends the reception desk. Brian has been directed to this organization. It occupies a simple building, overlooking a park filled with leafless trees. Brian had paused there, watched a dog running, its owner lagging behind. Squirrels as colorless as the sky. The trees had not yet budded. Annealed by sight, they were linked into a single chain of winter; the city is still trapped by it. January bares; everything is stripped for examination; diffident, proud, ashamed.

Brian waits for a counselor.

"The best thing in your case would be to apply for Conscientious Objector status; a case is now pending, so you might not have to base it exclusively on an organized religion's beliefs; but the closer you can get to that, the better . . ."

To repair an ancient machine, you need ancient parts. Organized warfare and religion; they grew together; they recognize each other's boundaries; their currency can be exchanged, their tariffs observed, their languages translated. It is here you need apply. . . .

"The personal references you have to get are important; it's helpful to have at least one of them with an institutional religious background . . ."

Dispensations, special pleadings, spiritual influence. The members of the Selective Service boards can be touched. Each reference is a point for them, to help locate you, somewhere off the path, lost in the wilderness. If your references are people of standing, pillars of the community, men of accomplishment, your case will be heard. They can be the lines that reach into your darkness and proclaim that indeed you have a center. He is sincere. Somehow, somewhere he contracted certitude. It is business legerdemain. They attest; they will cosign your conscience. You choose another absolute; it verifies their own. Nothing less will do. Tyrants all, the heart, the mind, the conscience.

"If you get your Conscientious Objector status in the works before you get your induction order you should be able to stall them for at least three or four more months . . ."

Stalled; the barnyard, holding pens, the tension of balance, a stance that is becoming intolerable to keep.

The counselor is thin and has a wispy moustache; he is full of cheer. It is behind him; he is proof of something. He has the zealousness of a returnee; he can do nothing less than repeat his accomplishment in others, for only that gives it meaning, importance.

It is also a job. He receives a phone call; it is a friend; he plans his evening over the phone. Dinner, a movie, someone to visit later. It is a lapse, as if the curtain had descended and he abandoned his portrayal. Hanging up, he resumes; his eyes glaze evangelically, brim with support.

"If all this fails, we know of a doctor . . ." he says and his eyes flash with salvation.

"Read this pamphlet," he says, "and if you want any help in filling out the forms when they come, get in touch with us again . . ."

Behind him a window's small panes mortise gray blocks of light; a tree branch's withered gesture. He turns away; Brian thinks of Major Sanjuaniwojimo. There is more than one way to skin a cat. We are all in the league.

The counselor severs the appointment with a glance at his wristwatch. Brian leaves. Another young man waits in the anteroom.

JACK STOPPED his bikecart when he saw Brian. A brand-new silver box, centered between two large spoked wheels. Jack was bundled in a pea coat, slapping his gloved palms together. His thinning blond hair shaped his head in senile disguise, Brian's age, he too balking at the draft, a boy from Michigan. He had lawyers working for him, complicated papers were being filed, letters of various kinds dispatched to his Michigan draft board.

"Hey, man, you've got to come by . . ."

Jack's invitation, a small white cloud, hangs in front of his face. His cart blocked a garbage truck which blared its horn. Jack twisted his cart to the curb and as the truck passed he covered it with abuse.

"Hey, motherfucks, haul your trash past," he said, with a mock-cripple's hilarious frenzy. "Where you been? Where you bound?"

"A little draft counseling; they sold me a booklet for a buck," Brian said, holding up the blue chapbook.

"Yeah, any help?"

"They lay out a method that hopes to discover or provoke 'procedural error,' to help you win in court; it seems filling the jails is no longer proper tactics; I don't know, they try to be helpful; can't hide that mortician's eagerness though, showing you the coffins . . ."

"Yeah, I know what you mean . . . gotta split . . . more serum for the dying," he says, pedaling into traffic, returning to the hospital where he works.

TIMOTHY HAD tied the inner door open and left an index card telling his guests that the party was three flights up. The smells of the hall had been Brian's first recognized breath of New York; it still held the scent of that time. Timothy had been the only person in the city Brian knew. They had once worked together at a summer theater. He put Brian up for the first few days when he arrived to begin school and had let Brian use his address for mail before he rented his room. Draft mail was still sent to Timothy's.

The party breached into the hall; guests chattered leaning on the banister. Brian went in the apartment's back door; a man was searching for his coat among those thrown down on the bed, sampling pelts freshly flayed.

"Haven't I seen you here before?" the well-groomed gnome asked.

Timothy had sent a telegram saying mail from the draft board had arrived, since Brian was without a phone. He threaded his way to the front of the apartment.

"Where am I singing now? I'm starving now . . ."

"With that hair and those sandals strapped up to her knees—well, my dear, she looked like a cross between Androcles and the Lion . . ."

"You know how that happened; they needed an in-one number; it was written so they could change the scenery; the result, a million copies . . ."

"I like Timothy's apartment; but I really think there's too much busy elegance . . ."

Brian found him leaning on the fireplace mantle; Timothy reached into his jacket pocket and handed Brian the envelope; he had covered it with novelty stamps: BULLSHIT. CAUTION: HAZARDOUS TO HEALTH.

"Get yourself a drink," he said, leading Brian to the liquor, "You know, Brian, there is a way out; it's a loophole the government leaves; not that there aren't plenty of homosexuals in the army; in fact, there was a base somewhere down South, Alabama I think, that they had to close, because the commanding officer was gay, as was his staff; he built it up by process of elimination and it was tough on the young men who ended up there . . . here," he said, giving Brian a drink, "insert finger and stir. If you want to become a *bona fide* fairy," he said, raising his eyebrows, mugging, trying to cheer Brian up, "that can be arranged . . ."

Brian shakes his head at Timothy who has kept a comic leer on his face.

"Well, I hear they give you a test; ask the names of

three gay bars operating in the city; then a vocabulary test: *dyke, basket,* that kind of thing; then some names of . . . correspondents . . . I guess they call them; I'm not sure it works; they take just about everyone now; they are *très* suspicious of imposters I hear, but you could bone up—excuse the coarse language. I was rejected because of sleepwalking, but that was ten years ago. I was in Julius's and three kids came in celebrating because one of them had just been refused by the army. They were all rather obvious queens, but it was on account of drugs, they said, not homosexuality; they sat around talking about their highs, about the blotters they took; I didn't even know what blotters were—did I feel old; one fellow didn't have to worry about the army since he didn't have any arms. When he left us for a moment I asked the others what his problem was. Thalidomide. You'd think he'd know better . . ."

"Thanks anyway, Timothy."

"Suit yourself, Brian; keep in touch; and if the FBI shows up here I'll invite them in for coffee and tell them you're thinking of joining the WACs," Timothy said, smiling, as a young man came up, took him by the elbow and stirred him back into the crowded room.

Brian could not bring himself to stay at the party, be its draft resister, declare noble intentions, articulate others' suffering, bay at the government's perfidy. Even if these people were otherwise, the somber and serious supporters of young men protesting the draft and the war, he could not present himself as an example of anything. He left, stepping across the tops of conversations.

". . . by the time we started to land I began humming 'Nearer My God to Thee' and read the index to the Bible for the third time . . ."

". . . the orchestra couldn't play too softly for Bruno; once he lifted his arms, to begin, then he hushed the musicians: *Too loud, too loud, pianissimo;* but the orchestra had not yet begun to play . . ."

The voices diminished like an opera chorus leaving a stage. The envelope from the draft board was in Brian's pocket; without its proof Brian would have doubted he had been there. Timothy had a commendatory plaque on his bedroom wall signed by the commanding general of the troops in Vietnam for his part in arranging a tour through the south of a roadshow company of a broadway musical. Christmas trees were stuffed upside down in trash cans. Slivers of tinsel still held to the branches. Newly fallen snow, dry as flour, hushed Brian's steps through the quiet named streets of the Village.

A SPASTIC sits across from him in the subway car, fingers fluttering. Brian stares at him absently and he takes notice, and with his trembling hand he seems to practice the fingering of a flute, to mask the affliction. Brian had read the letter:

Dear Sir: Your file was referred to the State Director of

Missouri after the receipt of your letter dated November 28, 1968, and further postponement is not granted. You have been afforded the same consideration as any other graduate student in your same circumstance. I might mention that you were notified in June 1968 that there were no graduate deferments except for those set out by the National Security Council last year. You were reclassified to class 1-A by unanimous vote. You will be notified by letter as to the date your are to report for induction in February. . . .

The sum of Brian's delays. A man asks to borrow a pen; he rides to Times Square practicing the signature on a credit card. He returns the pen as he leaves.

The car empties except for one other man sitting at the end of the bench. He begins screaming: "You might think you're something, but you're nothing but a bag of shit, you're nothing but a bag of shit . . ."

Slow as a turtle's head cautiously emerging from its shell, a thought comes to Brian to pick him up by his frail shoulders and stick his head out a window till a passing beam decapitates him. Just a thought. Brian is sick at it.

"You're nothing but a bag of shit . . ."

He stares at the letter.

"You're nothing but a bag of shit . . ."

At Seventy-second Street Brian gets off.

EIGHT

AN OLD MAN approaches Brian, beseeching, "Can I have a quarter, son, my check hasn't come as yet; I'd like to have coffee . . ."

Brian reaches into his jeans, shoves a fist through the complexities of compliance, his scholarship, his student loans. He looks beyond the man's damp eyes, overgrown with red vines, to semicircles of wrought-iron spikes that prevent passage from one building to another. A dull black prow prodding the blue sky. Feudal city, an old man waiting for a welfare check, needing a quarter to sup at a Formica trough. Brian's youth to them a slot machine and if they see apples spinning in bright eyes they'll get silver. I must look happy now, Brian thinks, for I'm not solicited often. He receives sympathetic avoidance. The sun is bright; the old man winces under its lash. Brian had not seen Audrey for a month; but she had called, arranged this occasion, a day to be spent in Riverdale with her brother and his wife and children. Her parents owned a house there they wanted to rent and her brother was spending weekends preparing it.

On Seventy-second Street a cobbler's window is filled with shoes, old and broken, the heap a death camp's rummage. A flat-bed truck is double-parked in front of a funeral parlor. *The Harlem Casket Co.* Three new coffins bake in the sun; a man in a doorway stares at them. Crowds cross the street with no regard to the traffic lights, testing the tolerances of the city. A bus lumbers to the curb; on a delta sits the subway's entrance; a newsstand fastened to its side. Men stand in front of it as at a long latrine ditch; a flesh deli, coldcuts—breasts, nipples, sliced away from the rest of the body. Unrequited desire is the hardest labor; it exhausted Brian. A movie house, an arrowhead-shaped park, Broadway and Amsterdam Avenue branch here. A bank, time, and weather, points of light connecting into numbers: 58°. Audrey should be here. 8:59. The day Brian rented the room was the first time he had ever been in the neighborhood. Before Jake had arrived. It hadn't seemed to him then so cheap and foul.

When he phoned Audrey this morning he was stirred by her drowsy mumble.

"Is it on?"

"Yes, it's on."

"Safe to see me in the daylight with the family."

A mad silence. Part of the truth. Audrey would not let

him touch her. Some decision had been made in which he had not taken part. He did not take; adhere, add to her.

They had been together only once on the West Side; they went to an old film, meeting Vanessa and Rhea there. Brian paid for their tickets and she made a face and pushed two dollars into his pocket. He protested. Spending the little money he had was like a criminal throwing away evidence. They went to dinner afterward, the two other women demanding that he be their guest. A Chinese restaurant in the nineties. The large room was decorated like a sinister Christmas.

They left, Brian hailed a cab; he felt himself to be a poor magician. It was the only thing he could summon up out of the night. After indecisive conversation by the curb he went with them; Audrey wanted to bid him good-bye there. Broadway fell away in gray decimals—eighties, seventies—till they passed his block, the portion of Broadway he wandered.

"It's an entirely different world here," Rhea said, not knowing it was Brian's neighborhood. Transient and shabby.

Audrey saw him less and less. A young couple moved in temporarily with her; they were a wedge, a convenient excuse. But that night Brian returned, wanting to remain; he followed her wordlessly up the five flights.

"I shouldn't even speak to you; I'm mad." They had spent the afternoon together; she wanted to wash her hair; she had to go to work early, off to her drawing board, clean, precise. Brian, she reminded him, had only classes to attend.

He beckoned her out of the bathroom and said goodbye.

"I'll call you," she had said, since he was to get a phone that week. Then the couple moved in.

Brian's ache for experience was equal to the amount he lacked. The simplest explanation for the way Audrey acted was for him the most difficult to comprehend. Though he knew her only recently, he was like a man, who, even though he can swim, finds himself in an ocean and then thrashes his arms—a catastrophe of possibilities.

"I suggest you get stoned immediately," she had said when he arrived one evening after the couple moved in. A record was playing Indian music. Audrey looked into a single candle's flame. Her face in shadows like the high vaults of a cathedral. Pretty hackneyed, he thought, the music, the candle flame.

"You don't realize how high I am; you'll have to treat me so carefully, I'm fragile . . ."

She studied the melting wax; it moved over the unsolvent wax like a column of marching ants.

"There I am," she said, "inside the flame . . ." It fluctuated in her breathing. Reverent hands of flame were reflected in her eyes.

"Look at him," she said, lifting her gaze away from the candle as a mother lifts a child from a cradle, toward the husband, one half of the couple, "Just look at him, how heavy he's become . . . I knew Ben would get heavy when he got high . . . wow! like the Rock of Gibraltar . . ." She laughed to herself, a deep laugh because it was light.

Brian wanted her to go off with him.

"You don't know how rooted to this couch I am."

"I know; it's your grandfather's couch; the roots go deep."

"I can't go with you," she said, her black sweater rumpling like a shell that is about to split, "Why do you want everything to happen so frigging fast? I'm the only rational one here, I see what's going to happen because I know where you're at . . . I've already thought about it; I think about it now . . . what do you really know? What do you really understand?" she said, leaning towards him without intimacy.

Brian left and hadn't seen her; but today she arranged. Safe in the daylight with the family. He could even try to forget the draft for the day; that had the patience of the Minotaur that knew eventually, no matter what path he took, he would finally have to cross his.

Broadway and Seventy-second. Nedicks. A movie house. How were they to get to Riverdale? Brian wondered. Where is Riverdale?

He could not stop recalling the few times they had been together. He was ridiculed by the memories: locked into the pillory of sex-remembered.

The evening after the first night she lay across his lap

allowing him to caress her body. Her housecoat was opened to the middle of its length and since he bore her up in his arms, its opening was stretched, and touching her breasts he didn't force the opening farther. His hand trembled with an apprentice's apprehension and after a long while he let it stray from her breasts like a parent's voice trailing off from the reading of a story since the child has fallen asleep. Her pink nipples were raised, the image on a coin. Sexual excitement in a woman often resembles the effects of being chilled.

He let his fingers slide down the isthmus of her belly and he placed his hand over her and pressed one finger down, a solitary note. It was as if his finger had broken into the bruise of a peach.

She bolted up and would not let him stay. But, how tender she could be, he thought now, the unexpected compliments, attributes he never considered having—even though they be lies a smile comes to him at their recollection.

THE SUBWAY bursts from the darkness as if it had taken flight. Hand prints and smears on the windows are revealed by sunlight as if the glass were photographic paper releasing its image with chemicals. At the wooden platforms on One Hundred Twenty-fifth Street they stop and from the concrete to their worn planks makes an alteration in time. The wheels on the rails sounded differently, the clacking over the suspended ties did not echo but fell away, pebbles down a cliff. Sunday had dispersed the crowds, the raised tracks dispelled the gloom, and Audrey dismissed the void, hoisted sails on his day. So much simple ignorance, he realized he had, like not knowing the local subway he so often traveled leaped from the underground out into the air, just one stop beyond Columbia University where he always debarked.

The train shut off completely. Wind rustles the trees; their tops, mossy stones, come up to the elevated station's platform. The doors are left open, a breeze enters. A newspaper flutters and falls. The sun grazes on the rough boards. Benches. A sign fades in the weather. Van Cortlandt Park. Voices bubble up from the street.

Audrey had pointed out the hill she climbed to the private school she had attended. He knew his attention was a burden to her; but she was lost to this station, the journey out here and back so often taken in her past; now, instead of going forward it seemed to be retreating. The past never makes the present any longer, nor does the future make it shorter.

"You're home."

"Yes, that's what I feel."

They walk down a length of crookback stairs, and around the rim of a park.

"We can either take a bus or walk, it's not too far,

except for these," she says, gesturing to the basket Brian carries, the bundle in her arms. It is hard for him to imagine Audrey any age than what she is, though as she glances at the short strand of stores across the street he knows she is seeing them with various eyes.

Four groups play baseball on the park's greensward; they wear laymen's haphazard uniforms; women and children fringe the peripheries. There is a rise of dark hills, a ridge of trees and great distance. An undamaged sky; no buildings mar it.

They stop at a grocery and are told they cannot buy beer since it is before noon; Brian is ready to believe it is a foreign law they obey and that this is an exotic village so changed is it for him. Curiosity makes him compliant. He is not annoyed and the storekeeper and his wife smile at Brian and Audrey and they return their smiles, laughing at the rule they all abide by, like parents amused at the mischievous antics of children.

It is residential; small homes, front yards; a young woman washes a car by the curb.

"I always wanted a yellow car," Audrey says.

"Had you stayed in Riverdale you would have one."

"I wanted you to say something like that."

"I should be able to pick your house out before you tell me which one it is."

The neighborhood grew like a tree; the outer rings of blocks are new, but as they walk deeper into the interior the houses rapidly age.

"Well, you failed; we're standing right in front of it."

Smaller than he had expected, perched on top of a hill; it has more land than its neighbors. Narrow steps, bleached wharf-silver, lead to it.

AUDREY TOOK him through the house in which she grew; her family had been renting it off and on and were about to again. They spent the day weeding and planting; taking off storm windows and putting up screens, preparing the house for the approaching spring. The house was white, except for the wood molding which was blond wood, coated with shellack, the color of Audrey's hair, of sailboat centerboards drying out in the sun. Her father was an architect, and her brother was about to be. He had one final examination to pass.

"Remember how I used to spit on you from here," Audrey standing on a porch said to her brother, looking down at him beneath her holding a rake. He blushed easily and Audrey laughed.

Brian and she went through the empty rooms, paused longest in her girlhood bedroom. Audrey described what was absent, the storms that had frightened her that she saw through the window her father had enlarged especially for her. The house was an ordinary one that they had altered;

interior walls disappeared, small windows replaced. It had been a dark house forced out into the light.

"Does your father think psychoanalysis has anything to do with architecture? Did this house need to be freed of its suburban psychosis?" Brian asked her, jokingly.

Audrey's childhood bedroom was a repository of awakenings. Since she had stopped sleeping with him, everything she showed him seemed to be a clue, the missing number that would open her closed sexual tumblers. Sunlight threw its warm sheet over her past in this room. Brian stared at its empty spaces the way he once stared at her bed from which he had been excluded while she had combed her hair before they went out. She shook her head disapprovingly and shut the door.

Audrey and Brian had gone to the theater, movies, walked the city, talked at length; experiences all on the surface, glancing off the life around them. And when Audrey stopped sleeping with him there was nothing remaining that had gone on between them. They had not made anything together, been linked by toil, or forged together by crisis or events—except by their intercourse. Without it little was left; for in the city that is what people do.

THEY BROUGHT her brother's son back with them. He and his wife and their small daughter took a cab back into Manhattan and since they would not all fit they parted, though everyone seemed to desire the stray hour of separation. They were to rejoin them later.

Walking to the subway their bodies gave up the day's accumulated heat. They waded through long shadows. The air above the subway platform was acrid with the tar the early spring sun had loosened in the ties. Brian, Audrey, and the boy sat in the last car with others who were also mottled with excursion fatigue.

Her brother's boy wanted to be held up to the car door's window to watch the retreating scenery. He was only a little younger than Brian's youngest brother and his quizzical suspicion of Brian—who he was, and what he was to Audrey—was the same as his parents', only more apparent.

He and Audrey had rested side-by-side in the sun when the boy came up and wanted Audrey to go off with him.

"You've been sitting too close to me," Audrey whispered as she went.

Exhaustion lessened his leeriness and he gladly assented to Brian's holding him up to the door's window; after a while he fell asleep and Audrey motioned to take him, but when they broke the damp bond that held them he awakened and wanted Audrey to hold him at the window.

The boy was wearing only shorts and a T-shirt, and resting on Audrey's hip his genitals were exposed. A walnut shell, a wrinkled peach pit, a tiny model of the brain's convolutions. The child in Audrey's arms, protective of her as a lover. Venus's boy.

And his sex, an indication of his power, a debt that you know will be called due. The boy, ineffectual in size, but complete as an abstraction. Why the pain? Brian wondered. Is that its source? All the aching that I've felt. Now, absent of feeling, he just stared at the awful futility they announced. Sexually abandoned, he felt like a patriarch, who, upon viewing his sons grown, now felt it appropriate to die. The child in Audrey's arms said: There are others, you are not necessary. The world rested on her hip.

The subway slipped beneath the surface; the light turned itself outside-in, the noise condensed, and with nothing more to see, they broke apart their pose, the ancient marble they had become.

Audrey was an unlikely auditor for this time in Brian's life; she was a young girl during the Korean war but it had touched her not at all. No one she knew or cared about had anything to do with the army or the protests against the war in Vietnam.

"I'm the silent generation, remember," she had said.

The inevitability of the draft foreshortened his life; and it made everything dear. The sense of loss was his constant companion. He thought Audrey considered him a good person to have around while she waited to fall in love with somebody.

"I'm tired," she announced, "I just want to go home and rest."

They had left her brother's and Brian had wanted to come with her. The benches near the bus stop were filled with an elderly, vanishing community. Once they were gone, they would not be replaced. It was to be an extinction. They had their childhoods in Europe and their dotages on benches along Upper Broadway. When they're gone no one will be left who will have made that arch.

"I've got to go," she said, as a bus veered to the curb, "I'll call YOU."

She walked through the bus with Brian staring at her, a bobbing seahorse in the aquarium green light of the bus. He went to his room, squinting into the sun that sliced down the side street, fighting back tears. He knew that if something could so easily conclude it had never truly begun.

NINE

"THE THING for you to do," he said, and Brian heard the office noises behind him, the background of desks and standing figures, the separate systems of conversation, distorting the information he gave like static, a serious intrusion, in that each voice diminished Brian's plight and the man's solutions, "the thing for you to do is call the head of Selective Service in Missouri and ask him to issue a postponement since you are applying for C.O. status; you have to exhaust all the administrative avenues, you have to give them every chance to reject you before you reject them . . ."

Brian tried to shape the lawyer from the palette of his voice; tie open at the neck, the confidence of knowledge, the security of process; hope is number, born of addition; progression begets faith.

"In court you won't have a good case unless you go through the physical and then refuse; they have to be given every chance to reject you; but if they do not postpone the induction order, don't show up; I will call them from here and explain to them how they should postpone . . ."

Not show up; the first real step, Brian thinks.

"That's right; they made his funeral a holiday, so that will complicate things. Call Missouri and get back to me before you appear."

Brian thanks him. The lawyer accepts it strangely, as if he had been mistaken for someone else.

Why do I hesitate to help myself? Brian wonders. He cannot stand to call Missouri to talk to the head of Selective Service. The name Brian was provided with, a general, stares up at him, a magic word he dare not utter. Postponement, dates changed, the shell game of time. They have all snapped, the ropes holding back the restrained animal.

Brian decides to call from his part-time job. Reach back through the maze of the country to its center, along phone wires, Ariadne's thread. I don't want to do this, he thinks, sick of the last-minute sandbagging.

He has abandoned the room to the cockroaches; he stopped killing them and they rejoice by coming out into the open, like a family running into the front yard after a storm has passed, looking up into the clearing sky.

He surveys the pitiable attempts to make the furnished room comfortable. The mortuary slab bed, the dresser, thick with aged varnish. A table he painted that never fully dried, the paint old and ruined. Gritty cinder dust scabs the windows' lips.

A small fist rasps at his door. Brian's next-door neighbor holds her alarm clock up to her shoulder, one hand behind it, ready to wind.

"Is it time to light the candles? What time is it?" she asks, adding words that Brian does not understand but is sure are endearments.

"Not yet; it's just three," he says.

He has never seen her out of her sour wrapper; how long has she been in her shroud, he wonders. Her white hair is plaited; her smile would frighten children, but her eyes have a kindness to which no one could be blind. She returns to her room cranking the large gears of her cheap alarm clock.

JAKE TELEPHONED. Lexa and he had returned from their honeymoon. They bought a truck with a camper and had gone to Alaska. Jake's father-in-law gave him a bear rifle.

Jake's hands burned with unspoken familiarity each night he prepared their camping site. All the meals he had eaten over outdoor fires. Crab meat and bananas, C rations bubbling in mess tin pots. He displayed to Lexa all his cloistered skills. In the woods, with a feral darkness covering them, memory annexed, Fairbanks and Da Nang were contiguous. Lexa had slept beside him in his mind through the Vietnam nights and now it was reversed; she was truly beside him, but in his dreams lived those black hours.

They returned from Alaska, filled with its glacial hollowness, sold their truck and camper, put the rifle in a deep closet and began their life together in the Middle West. They were to make a trip to New Orleans in April and they wanted Brian to join them there.

"If I can make it," he promised, thinking it unlikely.

Jake told Brian he was having a recurring dream. Brian and he were throwing a football in the street in front of their families' houses. It was the accumulation of all the twilights they had done so, while the sky around them darkened like the water of an agitated pond. The only sound was the wind threshing the treetops. The street is inclined, the space between them the longest distance they could toss the ball. The homes on the block are dark, except for the kitchens, which glow at their backs like fireflies' yellow lights. The street is empty. Two MPs appear, and take Jake by the arms, saying he wasn't finished yet in Nam, that he had to go back. Jake begins to kick and scream, yelling it can't be so. Brian stands up the block with the ball, ready to throw, his arm waving back and forth like a metronome. Jake, sweating, awakes.

Over the phone, his voice is lighter than it had been when he visited Brian. There was now some slack in it. Then, he recounted the stories as if they would disappear if he did not repeat them, here, in the World, as he had said soldiers referred to the States. In order to test them to see if they were real he had to transplant them in familiar soil. He felt for them the way amputees reach for their departed limbs.

Vietnam only seemed actual when he dreamt of it. And now the stories he told were not of Vietnam, but of his dreams of being there. His marriage stitched together the rent Vietnam made in his life, but it was still there, as if a distracted surgeon had left the scalpel behind, within the incision. Jake looked less frequently now at the slides and photographs he had of Vietnam; when he did, he felt strange and illicit doing so, as if he was consulting forbidden texts.

Brian and he laughed together, before hanging up, about Jake's decision, after twelve months in the jungles of Indochina, to mark the beginning of his marriage in the coldest climate he could discover. Alaska. They laughed. Alaska.

TEN

Brian had met her once before and tonight when he called she agreed to see him. Timothy was in Washington, touring and had let Brian use his place for the week; he had wanted to share its comforts with Audrey. The room on Seventy-sixth Street echoed his melancholia too well; cardboard boxes packed with books, clothes piled on the borrowed furniture. Timothy's apartment was like having a flashy car to drive for a date on a weekend. Oh, how he hated to acknowledge the comparison. Brian had relented, lost his resolve, tried to reach Audrey; her phone rang; sometimes, he knew, she did not answer it and if she did not answer it quickly she would not answer at all, except once when he had let it ring a dozen times and she snatched it up, her voice shattering glass.

He sits in Timothy's apartment, listening to the rain, tired from classes and work, still in damp clothes since he had been caught in the downpour. In his wallet he found the slip of paper with Lora Lee's number on it, some old raffle ticket you forget about till you discover you have won; he called; she remembered and agreed. It was the closest he had come to picking up a girl. Would Brian meet her since she wasn't familiar with the block? Yes. He did not want to bathe since he could only put back on wet clothes.

Where was Audrey? Who was she with? Had she left town? Dreary questionnaire thoughts. Sitting in one of Timothy's delicate chairs, the rubber poncho that served as a raincoat flared out, some motley airborne contraption that had failed. He was beginning to think of only a handful of hours at a time, and was beginning to realize that was what he was doing.

He left for the appointed time; the rain had stopped; it mulled the air. Down the street, the doorways, signatures of wealth, tall narrow windows, large plants growing in living rooms like trapped specimens. Free for the looking, the street was a long wand that summoned possessions. How strange, he thought, to be part of the enclave, to leave an apartment, the walls they present to the street, like those surrounding a besieged fortress, as runners gone off to fetch supplies. People leave their doorways guardedly, like a membership dispersing after secret meetings.

Doorways, dark cubbyholes, the shallow interiors of someone's shame. Doorways for passing out, pissing, for assault and protection, for hiding and lurking. Doorways are booths of despair and who first conceived of them, set back, slots of darkness, shafts of indecision, to linger, to peer out; doorways that emit only shadow; we all emerge from clefts.

Crossing Fifth Avenue, a church, spires with the intricate barbs of fishhooks, brown stone with a coat of velvet dust; cater-corner, a closed Longchamps, the gold letters on its white façade, a faded sun-blanched invitation. These sidewalks, as heavily traveled as the pathways of famous shrines. Streets of pilgrimage, that this city is, that takes so many strangers to its breast.

Walking east the wealth diminished. It faded more quickly than the day, which takes twelve hours to lose its light, whereas a half-dozen blocks is all that is needed to be put in the gray penumbra. Her building was built in the previous decade, of a white porcelain brick, which was now as dull as unattended teeth. What blindness did it take to construct white buildings in this city; like a sightless man dressing himself in riotous hues since he sees not at all.

Lora Lee wore a red dress and was carrying a Miami Beach straw basket of necessities, since she would be going to work the next morning. Her fire-red satin, a tube that empties itself after one application. She will burn herself out tonight and reemerge in the ashes of someone else's desire.

Lora Lee, a Siren plugged with the wax of some spermicide. Brian knew three or four others who called her, some strata of her life, separated by men. And what would it come to for her? he wondered. But tonight, dismissing as many of those thoughts as he could, letting loose ballast like a reckless balloonist, for tonight, he told himself, he wished not to give a shit. And he to her? They walked along, she displayed the umbrella she had, which folded itself to the size of a cucumber, then opened up like a black cabbage, then was stretched into a parasol which she twirled before them. A streetlight glowed weakly through it, a gray spot, a blind man's sun. Lora Lee had red hair, arranged in curls close to her head; her legs were like sharpened pencils: tiny ankles and calves, but wide thighs.

She was coy about the contents of her basket, not wanting to admit to the certainty of its evidence. Proof that something was to occur. Another couple passed them, nodding, as if couples were a separate species that took notice of each other; and it was true, for no couple ever acknowledged Brian when he walked alone. She suggested they go for a drink but Brian protested, assured her there was liquor enough where they were going. It was obvious to him she wanted to be taken somewhere, and he tried to be as entertaining as possible, till they reached Jane Street and into the building, the narrow stairs, the gamey horsehair smell of the carpet and to the door of the apartment. Lora Lee was visibly delighted by the way it looked.

What could she have expected, since the apartment did not resemble Brian at all, bespoke a life he did not lead, or that she thought of him to lead. By the way she turned her head, it seemed to him that she was excited by the place. Her response was to its smells, the fabrics, the tiny statues and trinkets, the *chatchkas* Timothy favored, the rugs, the fireplace. Wait till she sees the fur on the bed! Brian thought. It works, it all actually works! Timothy's decorating had done his wooing for him, though not much needed to be done.

IMAGINE SLEEPING with a woman and never getting a good look at her cunt! Brian thinks exasperatedly. It made him sympathetic to those who cannot remember the simplest things. Brian had never been able to investigate Audrey, but Lora Lee is an anatomical textbook.

Tag-end skin curled like spent flowers, salt-block and sedge and the same surprising first taste of the ocean. Aphrodite's sweat. Evolution trapped in amber scent; eons crossed olfactorily. Smell-feast, exhaled origins, musk-mint, tongue-taught, he laps: wakefoam bubbles on her fleshy crests.

"You shit."

Lora Lee reaches into her mouth with two fingers, a digital claw, bird's beak pincers. She had asked Brian if he liked asses. Brian was picturing orbs till he realized she meant holes.

Lora Lee sat on him, her back to his face, the rest of his

body received little attention or notice; a patient's draped body, only the area of operation revealed.

Two hands: She measured him like a horse.

"Do you like asses?" she asked and before he replied, "Sure," the stupid slur of assent, she began to lick his.

"You shit."

The digital claw, bird's beak pincers.

She returned to her ablutions. When did humans stop cleaning each other? he wondered. Grooming ritual, louse picked from scalps. Cleaning, it led to healing, cures, the birth of medicine. But now. Our beginnings make us as apprehensive as our ends. What was going on in her head? The disgust in her voice had altered, turned into expectation. It excited her; some snapped and broken logic, a world of reversed responses. With a midwife's pleasures she probed him with her tongue.

Brian could see his skin, picture its surfaces, on the mirror of her flesh. She developed it; the shape of desire; rubbing him against the roof of her mouth, the place it defined was the ribs and spine of a great fish.

"See for yourself," Lora Lee says, haggling carnal wares, and Brian bends back her flesh and looks at it; a small pit of gray dust. The shape of the smudge of ash that he had had put on his forehead for sixteen years.

"What do you think?" she asks as he nudges it.

If ever there was a place, this is it, Brian thinks. Timothy's Vaseline, in readiness, next to his hand-held hair dryer in the medicine cabinet. Buggery's blush, the red rash he displayed padding through the apartment naked. Or was it the innocent pressure from sitting? Brian suggests a shower, the implied lubricity, but Lora Lee demurs, says she doesn't want to wet her hair. They let it pass and rest.

Shackled with lust, all the erections Brian has had little use for, it does not abate. She sits down on top of him on the morris chair. She makes grimaces of pleasure which in their overdrawnness he knew were for his appreciation. What looking-glass taught her that popping of eyes and pursed lips, her tongue beating around her mouth like a spatula cleaning out the rim of a bowl, was a show of delight? It probably expressed something once, but now it was garbled, a message passed along by too many mouths.

He liked her weight around him; it fixed him, gave him a place. He put his arms under hers and stood up. In her he had found a center of force; they were lever and fulcrum. She seemed weightless now, locking her ankles around his back, arms encircling his neck. Brian walked about the room, then headed back to the bedroom. He knocked her knee going through a doorway; then, with a little leap, they plummet onto the bed, actually happy for one moment together, their shared mirth like the trail a falling star briefly shows.

"Brian," Lora Lee said, without irony or mockery, "you are all man." He cringed, though he knew that in some catalog of phrases you are likely to hear in a lifetime, that was one.

But, both in their fall, they recognized for a second some actual combination of themselves, if only a mass dropping through nothing together. And her knee that Brian banged, had that been a cloud of celestial gas, the collision might have fostered a galaxy.

ELEVEN

The Conscientious Objector form arrived:

1. Describe the nature of your belief which is the basis of your claim. . . .

There are five lines on which to write; the space is monumental; its whiteness is blinding.

Describe the nature. . . .

Sitting beneath his parent's bedroom; above him muffled copulating noise. The bed creaks under more than restless sleep's labors. There are many children; surely the union above will not account for another. His mother has long since passed into the fixed state of a haggard mother-of-eight.

It is as if he is witness to his conception some twenty-one years ago; did the springs jump then with more abandon? Has their passion, stretched out along the arc of his life, diminished or excelled? Is his heart as warm as the amount theirs' has lost or gained?

Describe the nature. . . .

His mother takes in his father who then is the age of Brian now; desire once required no innovations; both fresh high-school graduates, coming of age during a world war, going straight from their childhood homes to their own connubial one. No space: Matrimony was both freedom and bondage.

Brian, fluid suspended mite, pre-human, a biological stage, in company of an unmated thousandfold swarm, is knighted with ego when he crowns himself on her egg's fecund periphery—becomes, like chemicals mixed in a phial, another substance: human, an embryo, fetus, invisible to the eye. Barnacled to his mother's organ, with no more thoughts than a bivalve, he develops.

Describe the nature. . . .

He is unlooked for though not unexpected; he staunchs his mother's flow; he is marked by the absence of blood. He does not recollect celebrations or despair. His lineage goes back as far as anyone's.

He knows he is his father's son for he leaves the bathroom stinking with the same exact scent as he; they smell alike. There is no denying the distinctiveness of fragrance. His father does not go into the army during World War II. An eye defect is the cause. He works in an airplane factory; he carries with him a slight shame that he was refused by the army.

Brian listens to them above him; he feels his randomness.

. . . state why you consider it to be based on religious training and belief . . .

A bawling infant is held over a marble bowl; annointed, splashed upon, tongue touched with salt, brow marked with oils, christened, broken into society, acknowledged, provided with surrogate parents, linked to a community, named for a saint, cast into a tradition, given roots. I baptize thee in the name of the Father, the Son, and the Holy Ghost. . . .

2. Explain how, when, and from whom or from what source you received the religious training and acquired the religious belief which is the basis of your claim. (Include here, where applicable, such information as religion of parents and other members of family; childhood religious training; religious and general education . . .)

He was the oldest son of a large family and if his father and he had been required to learn a foreign language in order to talk to one another it would have required but a short study. He can recall two early conversations with his mother clearly. One, sitting on the steps of the second home they lived in, she explaining the French she knew: *Je t'aime* (acquired from her brother's time in France during World War II); and when she told him why his older sister did not have to do the dishes certain nights and that he had to do them. Because of her menstrual pains. His mother's explanation was as cloudy as the television image he was watching and she took as the summation of her talk the gas company slogan that had just been offered: As you travel, ask us.

In most matters he grew up unquestioningly as corn. His father, in an introduction to the world of business, would take him along on deliveries he would make to plants, bringing them the small part that was causing their machines to be idle until it was replaced. They would walk down the echoing aisles in the gloom of the night shift and the foreman would take from his father the tiny bearing, wrapped in brown wax paper; as they left the vast hangars that housed the machinery, great engines, they would sometimes start up, because of the part that had just been brought and this is the reason he was taken along, to see his father bring them deliverance.

Brian was born in Chicago, the year World War II ended, but only remembers the visits there with his paternal grandparents who lived across the street from the mills of United States Steel. Throughout the night, in a room baked with the leaven of linoleum smells, he watched the reflections of the smelting furnaces in the glass of a neighbor's window. An orange flame pulse that twitched like exposed muscle of a lab dissection. The dull thunder of the smelting would wrinkle the nights he lay in a white metal bed surrounded by wreaths of rosaries on the corners of his grandmother's mirror; and under her bureau's glass top was pressed a life's cache of holy cards.

His family is superficially Roman Catholic; no theology disturbs their belief. And it is superficial religion and bigotry which is the hardest to depose, for it is always near the surface.

The front yard of his grandparent's home was sunken and sandy; it grew thick with tall weeds on livid purple stalks. There was a pay phone in the dining room; the large table, used only for occasions, was covered with yellowing linen brought from Ireland by his grandmother. A plum tree in the side yard produced only sere fruit. He delighted in the big bottles of orange soda and the white weisswurst that would explode in boiling water and belly up like an exhausted whale.

Christmas would find a relative dressed in a rented Santa Claus suit; all the accumulated children would receive a gift. His grandmother booked steerage passage aboard the *Titanic* but delayed her departure to be able to travel with a friend. His grandfather worked through the depression with the railroad; an alcoholic, he battled with his wife, who—amongst Brian's earliest memories—would pour his rye down the kitchen sink, driving him onto the streets and into hospitable bars. Brian, at times, would accompany him during the day, perched on a barstool next to him, drinking grape juice. During one of these walks he splashed water on his grandfather's trousers and every year of his life Brian was to know him, he would hear that piece of insolence recounted. His wife, Brian's grandmother, well preceded him, having committed herself to a demented rocking chair and aimless walks. Not as pliable as he, she broke earlier.

Brian's father discovered that the middle class required a strong ethnic bleach when they moved to Kansas City; Chicago was a divided ghetto town, but in Kansas City plain white Americans fare better as good fellows, with common interests, and though a Catholic boyhood was all he knew, he had no conception of being Irish. Whatever was shed was not replaced and it made little difference to him. The country raised him, more than his parents, and recollection of television households are as acute as those of his own relations.

He moved on to Cub Scouts, baseball, and had his first Holy Communion; there are home movies of that, of Brian in white short pants, walking stiff-legged, dimpled knees and a big head. In color. He has no real memory of it, only the recollection of the film. At the same time his eyes widened before the televised scenes of mass burials at concentration camps; not so much at the mounds of bodies, but at the black spade of pubic hair on the corpses, their flaccid breasts. Talk of lye, clods of earth, bulldozers driven by Americans fearful of plague.

His boyhood world was separated into blocks. The Fifty-seventh Street boys and Fifty-sixth Street boys had divided themselves into gangs that fought each other at their common intersection; the manhole cover was the black sun these confrontations orbited; but they were decided upon mutually, the rules and limits of intervention, the style of warfare. First, it was cavalier, medieval tunics found in basement ragbags, broadswords of broomsticks; coffee cans guarded knuckles, and shields were made from apple-basket lids.

A half-dozen on each side. The passing motorist would see twelve youngsters battling each other with broomsticks, the tiny crowd surging from one side to the other, sticks flourishing. After chasing each other through backyards, they would go off to repair the swords or to display cut knuckles, injured by their own coffee can handguards.

Tiring of that century they moved on to air warfare; they tried all forms, charted an ontogeny of conflict. Divided into Russians and Americans they set to building armadas of plastic airplanes, constructing detailed airfields in backyards. Yellow dust of a barren garden was the earth of Japan—they imagined American bases there; a damp garage served as a Russian field, equal to the muddy climate of the Steppes. They would meet at the intersection, now a hot pacific of asphalt, and run at each other with the plastic planes, spitting out machine-gun fire, protesting maneuvers if they seemed too impossible, quarreled over who was actually shot down. This continued till raids on the backyard airfields stomped out runways, damaged cardboard hangars. The end came when the Americans flew at the Russians with plastic biwings, calling out, "Zitt, Zitt," claiming they were shooting invisible electric rays.

At thirteen they drifted away from their neighborhood, joining up with larger gangs whose games consisted of shooting at each other with Daisy air rifles, around Brush Creek, a cement drainage canal that ran through the southern part of the city. Black leather jackets and motorcycle caps with winged wheel emblems sewn on the front, a white strap of vinyl creased the tops.

For twilight amusement, waiting to be called in for dinner, they would throw daggers at each other, aiming between spread-apart legs. German daggers that fathers had brought back from the war. The quality of the steel intrigued them, the emblems on the handle, the trench running down the blade that was known to be the outlet for flowing blood.

Older boys discovered magazines that were guarded and shown, but never loaned out; Brian saw an adult woman's genitals for the first time one night, lit by the interior light of a fifty-eight Chevy convertible. A full page thicket of pubic hair, in color, with a brown crease running in the middle, looking like an unflowing, but still muddy, riverbed.

At that time, a friend got a pack of playing cards which they examined in a closet together; black and white pictures, women gripping men, one woman on a bed with her legs apart, the tail of a large lizard inserted in her. Hot and flushed he became, though not knowing what to attribute it to, anymore than to blame the bare bulb heating the small, airless closet.

Not instructed by anyone, and surprised by the discovery, he began masturbating. Too ashamed to buy magazines at a neighborhood drugstore; what could a twelve-year-old want with a man's magazine except for self abuse! Brian discovered in his family's *Encyclopædia Britannica*, the section "Painting" and so, with a heavy buckram volume propped open before him he swooned over Delacroix and Titian. The lust of a thirteen-year-old does not diminish and you are wild to couple with anything.

He went to the parish grammar school, the halls lined with large class portraits, oval sepia photos. As the classes year-by-year grew in size, the individual photographs shrank. A parish priest would twice be summoned to instruct the children for an hour on their faith. A small flag jutted from the wall; take any ten children and have them recite the "Pledge of Allegiance" and it will sound the same. They were divided by sex and size. There would be holy-day processions; tiny female children marched with pagan flowers in their hair.

In the half-basement of the school a hundred children ate lunch. Small barn-shaped tin pails, thermos bottles, wax paper, brown bags, single pieces of fruit. Dwarf milk bottles with thin cardboard stoppers. The children sat on benches at long beaverboard tables in the dark green room, sunlight entered acutely and bordered the floor on two sides. Brian ate here five days a week, thirty-five weeks a year for eight years. The smell has been worn into him.

He was an altar boy and served six-thirty mass, never

learning the Latin exactly. He'd ride bundled on a bicycle through the winter mornings, arriving at the sanctuary door; the room was warm, thick with incense, burning beeswax candles, the sharp vinegar smell of the first-press wine. Pebbled tongues, long rows of communicants, tongues lime-coated white, the pressing down of the host, the indentured "Hoc Est Corpus Meum." One after the other, the morning procession, red crosses stitched into the starched white corners of the communion cloth. He has seen a thousand arched tongues waiting for a wafer of dust.

Riding downtown with his father at that age, from the outskirts of the city, enjoying the cool rush of the night air, the lights of the small dials of the car's instrument panel were the constellations he knew, his father made an infrequent extemporaneous remark, "You're bleeding."

And so he was. Brian looked into the silver wing of the rear-view mirror, a large boil beneath his eye had burst. The only public burden he carried from puberty was an unhealthy complexion. It introduced him to pains, real and imagined. From a drugstore on Troost Avenue he stole remedies since he was embarassed to purchase them. He did it so regularly that he was sure the shrunken pharmacist must have known of his larceny.

Such concoctions that those creams and unguents were, seemed to be products of natives still given to cures of mixed dung and leaves. At night, going to sleep with his face smeared with this mortal clay, its sulfureous fumes lead him to believe the folklore his relatives told him, "Oh, look at the evil spring out on Brian's face."

When it did not lessen after three years and he was sixteen, he was sent to a doctor at his own feeble request and from the dawn of civilization, the primitive mixtures of home cures, he was transported to its current edge, and administered X-ray treatments from sidereal machines, that did nothing but hum, while he lay outstretched, parts of his head shielded with heavy rubber, lead plates over his eyes as if he had already passed away, while the doctor and his assistant retreated behind a protected door. The electric hum was the only indication that anything was happening, that the tubular appendages of the contraption were alive, the hum an incantation that he's afraid probably worked too well.

He was never free from it and he cursed his affliction, most often because of its minorness, never understanding why the fifty-six square inches of his face had to be tormented, and that its small area mattered so much.

Whenever he gets a sunburn, he appreciates anew the minute tolerances of the universe and realizes again that the smallest weights and distances cause immutable changes, and so, he is sure, that his bad complexion was a hand on his back that guided him but little, but guided nonetheless.

NOTICE—*Imprisonment for not more than 5 years or a fine of not more than $10,000, or both such fine and* *imprisonment, is provided by law as a penalty for knowingly making or being a party to the making of any false statement or certificate regarding or bearing upon a classification (Military Selective Service Act of 1967).*

Brian throws the forms on the floor, where they lay, a large stunned seabird.

TWELVE

WHY WOULD anyone want to go to prison? Brian wonders. To be a paragon, an exemplar? Draft cards had been burned, organized ceremonies in Central Park, the thin paper curling into ashen scrolls. Every war sees these examples; a medicine's unlooked-for side effects. The Oxford oath: Hell no, we won't go. Is that the part I am to play? There were resisters in jail, he knew. Us or them. Join. Publicity worked the miracle of the loaves and fishes: one into many. A private act made public becomes political. Us or them. Join. Conviction; that would be the reason and that would be the result.

Jake and Brian had registered for the draft together; they turned eighteen the same month. Each sat at desks answering the clerks' dry questions. Eighteen. The small white card was a necessity, a sought-after ticket. They now could buy 3.2 beer across the state line in Kansas. A draft card was the proof of age accepted. To celebrate they

did just that, drove over to Kansas, flashed their new draft
cards. "Draft cards for draft beer," Jake had said. Birth-
rights are cheap. Freshmen in college, healthy and brash,
they toasted each other. Four years come and gone; Jake, a
year in Vietnam.

The draft had been a canker of preoccupation for Brian
since nineteen sixty-four; it had become part of him,
something his flesh had enveloped. Its presence would be
sharply felt only for a moment; daily it was a dull cradled
pain. In sixty-four he had written a letter to his draft board
refusing to be inducted; it was never sent. He had dropped
out of college then, but had returned, in order to reclaim a
deferment. It was the year the Selective Service gave
national tests to male students; he had scored sufficiently
high. And so, he was deferred; but finally it has worked its
way to the surface, become inflamed. Thinking quietly
about it now, giving reasons, seemed as foolish as talking
about fire and its properties, while standing at the center of
a conflagration.

THE CITY's population, when you are alone, is the
surface of an ocean that buoys you up; you thirst for what
surrounds you. Wander and you are part of the dance of
the city's night. It is all that is left when you have no
money, no one to visit. Solitude is poverty's most ardent
mistress. The legs move blindly, draw you onto the streets.
And they are the city's bowels, which nourish and empty

it. They twist back on themselves. There is more margin here. And to it cling the desperate, the flint-eyed madmen, the diseased, the jagged fringe. Street corner oracles, deprecating the cosmos, chant the cabal language of gone minds. There is room for them here: frayed lives caught and held in the tangled edges of the city.

A young girl waits at the bus stop. One leg is withered, the other flawlessly shaped. Its perfection sharpens the loss of the other. Brian stares at her. It is impossible to feel sorry for one's self, there is always a more deserving creature at your side. Though I won Audrey once, he thinks, it continued to be my way of losing. No one, he understands, wants to hear about his troubles with the draft. It is like listening to people who boast of their infirmities.

Everything is suspended, seems withheld to him; he has shaped his life around it. The room he took because it could be abandoned; all jobs are temporary.

You can sometimes desire solitude, but you never can have a passion for it. Walking the streets at night he sees men crumpled in doorways, caught by the flood of unconsciousness, in the desperate poses of frozen flight: citizens of new Pompeii.

At Astor Place a police bus is parked in the shadows of Cooper Union Square. Police wait for a disturbance, some planned raid, play dice in the aisle.

Down Houston Street Brian sees across the pavement a large black woman, three hundred pounds of shadow under a street lamp's cloud, screaming at an old man collapsed beneath her. Two companions tug at her great arms.

"I'm going to piss right on that white man's face . . . I'm going to piss right on that white man's face . . ."

The two people with her, a man and a woman, try to get her to come along with them.

". . . piss right on his face . . ."

She parts her coat and lifts the hem of her dress as if she is going to fan him, revive him. The stop light changes and cars fill the street, shut off the scene.

At a White Tower at Seventh and Greenwich Brian eats. A young man comes in and sits three stools away. He orders two bowls of beans.

"And I want two BOWLS, not two cans in one bowl; last time you gave me one bowl and I'm not sure you put two cans' worth in it."

"All right, all right, two bowls, two bowls," the short counterman says.

"You have to pay me," the counterman says, pushing two bowls in front of him.

"Later," the young man says, spooning beans.

"Now."

"Now, PLEASE!" he says, furiously, picking up a bowl of beans, ready to hurl it at the counterman.

The counterman backs up against a glass case full of pie

slices and grabs a wooden club from beneath the counter.

"It'll be assault," he says, "if you come across that," he says, indicating the Formica.

They scream at each other; Brian chews his food.

"I'm just back from Vietnam," the young man says, as some sort of explanation.

"No you're not," the counterman yells back, "your hair is too long."

They continue to yell; Brian eats. The young man dares the counterman to come out and fight; the counterman dares the young man to come across the counter and fight. Their line is smeared with ketchup, barriers of sugar pots, napkin holders. The threats subside; the young man returns to spooning the brown beans.

"Oh, my arm, my arm," a man moans on Eleventh Street. Another stoops to help him.

"Let's get you to the hospital."

"I just came from there," the man on the sidewalk groans, "they wouldn't help me."

"Let's try again," the other says.

"Leave me be," the man cries, filling the block with his lamentation, "Just leave me be."

The samaritan departs; the moans fill the street.

On the Sheridan Square subway platform Brian waits for an uptown train. A woman wearing a cardigan sweater put on backwards wanders, repeating, "I spit blood." She stops and examines herself in a gum machine mirror. "I spit blood."

Walking dejectedly back to his room after midnight, Brian sees her coming toward him, a dim figure. Her gait is a flag of distress. Rather than cross the street, make that wide arc of disapproval, Brian continues straight ahead. Her person is a catalog of misfortune; her past was lamed, her left arm stiff; she is garbed from the haberdashery of waste cans. The sounds she mutters are not language. In her right hand she carries a rolled-up umbrella.

As they draw near some bleak radar she has equipped herself with went off; she begins to make repelling noises, for it was she who was truly alarmed. She had learned to strike first, before being struck. Had all those missing teeth been shaken loose? She drew back her umbrella in a gesture that a million years of evolution had made lovely. It had the grace of a scorpion's coiling tail. It seemed to Brian that he was being attacked by bats; he dodged her fury, went past her, and on up to his room.

THIRTEEN

"WELL, ONE of two things is going to happen. I'm either going into the army, or I'm going to refuse induction."

"I thought I said I'd call you," Audrey had said when she recognized his voice. "It's your choice," she said. "What do you expect me to say? Watching you make up your mind about this is like watching the thrashings of a dying fish. I just wish you'd stop browbeating me with it."

"All right; I will; good-bye."

"Good-buy-I."

If I've decided anything, Brian thinks, hanging up, it's never to call that bitch again.

FOURTEEN

"Hurry, or we'll miss the afterglow . . ."

The artist and Brian hold the painting pressed alongside the speeding taxi's side. Wrapped in plastic sheeting, pedestrians see a pastel abstraction racing up Park Avenue. It would not fit in the cab; they were delivering it. The purchaser rode along, through the dusky troughs of the city. Driving through Central Park, the artist and Brian hold onto the painting's frame through the cab's windows as if it were a shield. The driver smiles, foreseeing a large tip. There is a moment when street lights and skylight are equally bright; they are in focus, the sky loses dimension, flattens, and the street lights and sky blend, balance like fruit hung in its tree.

The purchaser's apartment, she had explained, was rung by a terrace from which the entire city could be seen.

"Even though the sun will be down we can still catch the afterglow . . ."

"Are you interested in film?" the purchaser had asked him when he arrived at his part-time job; she approached him from behind a movie camera's bank of blinding lamps. Brian was employed by an artist who was being evicted from her studio; she had fought her eviction and had won a series of delays. A business wanted to expand and it had bought the building.

"Mafia money," the artist said, "the landlord calls himself a doctor; a doctor! A Sicilian dentist."

He arrived with his lawyer, to assure himself that she was vacating. A tiny man in an incandescent blue blazer and white patent leather shoes.

"He's nothing," the artist said, "just their front man."

The landlord and she argued; he became agitated, his olive face reddening. He began to pump his arms up and down in a furious march. His lawyer, a large doughy man, tried to calm him. They left with the Sicilian dentist trailing threats.

The artist, the purchaser, and Brian then set off for Central Park West. The sinking sun turned the windows of the delicate shops of the east side streets to a shimmering mercury.

"I just moved in," the purchaser said, "don't mind the furniture, I had to buy it from the previous tenant."

Her terrace was a horseshoe around one of the building's towers.

"Manhattan, c'est une île," the artist said, standing with Brian at the railing. The city's rivers, steel-gray callipers, grip the land.

"We're getting a little afterglow," the purchaser said. Orange and red radiance filled the streets, outlining the buildings. They stared down at the guttering light, surveying the city like survivors; the afterglow: livid and dying.

"If you have to live in the city, you might as well live like this," the purchaser said, indicating all that was below them. Along the western horizon a pink band subsided like a fever.

Window lights begin to glitter against a black mantle; urban constellations, the pattern of lights its buildings make—the beast logic: graphs.

All this will I give thee. The city provided these moments. A man sat on a shore trying to comprehend an ocean; a person in a clearing looking up at stars; a young man on a Central Park West terrace viewing New York City. I am separate from them, Brian thinks, the millions beneath and around me; tomorrow, I join some young men at Whitehall Street. Tomorrow, my life parts, will be diverted. I dash myself against rocks. So, tonight I'm shown what I'm up against. C'est une île. An amoeba, a cell, reducible infinitely. Stop anywhere and the distance forward will equal the distance behind. Standing on the rim, looking down; now, someone has died, just then a birth, a womb quickened, a uterus scraped: tears, laughter.

How much can the eye circumscribe? Bombs are falling, limbs cascade, tumble in a fiery wave. Here is stillness, there chaos. And tomorrow, another pebble into the sea. The merest ripple. I before the examiners.

"Brian," the artist sweetly calls, "it's time to go."

FIFTEEN

Brian returned and discovered that his next-door neighbor was moving. She had lived alone in her room for over two decades, moving in when the brownstone lost its domestic autonomy and was split up into cells. Her rustling knock had become familiar to him, a dry branch against glass. She had given him jars full of borscht, thick with beet parings. It was as new to him as everything else he had first encountered here. All he had done for her was to open stuck caps, tell her when it was time to light her Sabbath candles, and occasionally plug in her heating pad. She startled him the first time, after he connected the pad, by taking his hand and kissing it—the homage of the poor.

Her sister, younger than she, somewhere in her sixties, met Brian in the hallway when he returned. Cardboard cartons were stacked outside her door. She was moving, he was told, to a project on the Lower East Side. She had been attacked recently, an evening Brian was out. A man came through her room's cyclopean window. He took her purse, struck her, and left through the door. Brian's landlady had told him the tale.

She had not knocked on his door since and now she was leaving. Her sister asked him if he wanted to buy a table. She opened the door and there she sat, thin white hair wrapped round her head like excelsior. The table was brown enameled metal.

"Ten dollars," the younger sister said.

At the table she did not look up at Brian; her stare reached beyond him; he was lost in her foresight. She seemed not to recognize him. Beneath her eye was a chevron of purple bruise.

"The project will be better for her," the sister whispered into Brian's ear. She was younger, but for him, it was like distinguishing between the Bronze and Iron Ages.

"There are guards . . . five dollars?" she said, smelling disinterest.

Brian felt like kissing the old woman's hand; his slight inclination towards her pierced her sight and she started. Her fear erased his impulse. She turned her head back slowly, till it remained in rigid profile; the bruise ran down the side of her face like dark wax.

"Tell her good-bye for me," he said to her sister and went on his way.

SIXTEEN

A NAME, a number, an address. A call is made; an appointment is arranged. Eleven o'clock; the day's penultimate hour. A psychiatrist.

Brian's parents once threatened to send him to their parish priest, to work some homely exorcism, such a stranger he was becoming to them. Deep into adolescence, he battled with his older sister. How much skin had he lost under her fingernails? he wondered. The priest was to calm him, a truculent fourteen-year-old. The visit was never made; its specter was a sufficient quieting spell. A psychiatrist was ever a more mysterious personage.

Brian's room is a cranium space; he cannot flee his thoughts or it. It is a map of his discouragement; the bathroom his sex life, the two-gas burner his hopes, the stunted icebox his ill-fed stomach. He has come to New York and it has handed him this scrap of paper. Nowhere else would he have found it. A name, a number, an address. Who holds the key? A psychiatrist. The draft is the culmination of his youth. To go in or not to go in; choose. The joylessness of preventive measures.

"It's so different when there is no possibility," he recalls Audrey saying, "when nothing can happen." She had looked down at herself, puzzled. "The Pill is great; I'm just being crochety; crotch-shitty," she said, punning. Anal-list, Brian thinks, him-bare-assed.

Just as easy to have been caught like Jake, he thinks, flowing out of the Midwest into the army. This tributary did not intersect his; but it has mine. The fork: a name, a number, an address.

The army is a recessive gene, a throwback trait he carries of the culture; a pact made with the state by history. Reappearing now: serve.

There are many forms of envy and a kind most biting is when we covet another's errors and wish that we could have committed them.

Jake did not balk; the army was a way out. Trapped in the familiar, it took him from what he knew. The shock was that he could return. "The trouble, Brian," Jake had told him, "is that you can go home again."

Brian awakened from a childhood like a man from amnesia. Chronology has been violated; his first eleven years could have taken place anytime in the twentieth century; but his adolescence was marked and now he is fixed and the ages flow around him. The only way to relinquish the urge to do something is to be able to imagine it fully. Television's test pattern has been the print of the nails. I have seen it. Is nothing evident? he wonders. Do we as a species pass on knowledge less effectively than peas?

PARK AVENUE's face is reflected in its doormen. Suspicious, subservient to wealth, scornful of the poor; stuffy, worried with appearance, maintaining a bought neatness, satisfied with shared proximity. A servant is the parody of his master. Brian arrives at the building and the doorman responds with an empirical smirk. He knows the kind of people the doctor sees. A Park Avenue psychiatrist. The elevator rises. I am being brought before the Wizard, he thinks, the wonderful Wizard.

"Well, I could have you committed."

The word breaks through Brian's stupor. Committed. I am not committed, so I can be committed. He is taken aback. Committed? A hospital, sanitarium. Declared incompetent, insane, locked up with zanies. Roving eyes, lolling jaws, the extravagant faces of the deranged fill his mind.

"I'm sorry," Brian says, "I don't have any money . . ."

"Oh, there wouldn't be any money involved; you'd go to the city hospital, Bellevue . . ."

Oh, he thinks, Bellevue! Bedlam, white smocks, a tin

plate on his left arm. This *is* crazy, Brian thinks. He wants out, but he does not want out that badly it seems.

"That's the only certain way . . ."

The doctor had asked Brian what he wanted.

"They are quite suspicious of general psychosis; it has to be something terribly specific . . ."

The steps are few and each one drastic.

"Just to say, for instance, that you are suffering from severe depression—which well might be the case—or are suicidal," he says, eyes questioning, "given to distortions, drug-induced psychotic episodes? All common enough, is not sufficient . . ."

Brian sits in a straight-back chair, sees the pallet couch, bookshelves, gilded editions, framed diplomas, thinks of Hippocrates.

"Have you ever had any homosexual contact?" the physician asks somberly.

Contact? Brian thinks. He is looking for something that could pass for the truth. Contact? Timothy. He knows to inquire what he means by *contact* would cut off the path.

"Yes."

"That's second best; I'm not sure it will do the trick, but . . ."

He writes at his desk and fills two sheets of letter paper. He puts it in an envelope and seals it. He hands it to Brian.

"Aren't I to see what it says?"

"No; it might disturb you."

On the envelope is written: FOR MEDICAL EXAMINERS ONLY.

"And, if you should decide that you want to be committed, call my service."

SEVENTEEN

THE MIDDLE WEST is redundant; its flowers are not riotous and varied; they fill fields, copy upon copy. The wind brushes acres of wheat like a hand smoothing velvet; machines thresh and bail, grain is the dust of life, uniform as sand. Number does not frighten people for they are used to repetition. Cattle, chickens, the fowl of meadows, fish strung on lines—growth grown only for harvest. Seasons are distinct, snow recedes, dank spring prepares, summer dries, fall makes fertile again. The Middle West breeds surrender, a pride in succumbing. No boy rushes more eagerly to war than one who can drop his hoe. Watching crops rise and fall as regularly as the tides implants deeply drawing up and release, the pull to answer calls, summonings, the continual beckoning.

How many afternoons, if he dawdled, did his mother say, "Come when you're called."

We are all conflicted. The moon, our hearts and minds,

brings us near then lets us go. We are all divided. The blood is released by constrictions and relaxations: The interrupted pulse tempers resolve.

Why am I still torn? he wonders. Fear? A ring without a gap; there is no direction in which it can be avoided. The army, jail, and now this sealed letter. An unexpected element, unlooked for, a third thing, a triangle, the symbol of magic and necromancy. Army. Jail. The Letter. Three sides that are proportional to their magnitudes.

And what do I want to do? He knows he is able to go into the army. And Jail? It too is possible; there are people in the wings. Only those who never think they will enter a prison are deterred by the thought of one.

It seemed a perversion to extract from the war the chance to prove one's self righteous; there was, he sensed, something seamy in being pure amidst its foulness. To be sent to a minimum security workfarm for two years or more, to be locked away: suffering, yes, a life possibly ruined, but still retaining that spike of certainty in the eye. I have done what is right. Right because there was an elegant alignment of reasons and circumstances and that arrangement would be achieved as infrequently as a simple eclipse. For a moment. Then it would seem wrong; and then right. Then wrong. Caught in the sway of heavenly bodies, forever.

Who am I struggling against? The State? Where is the enemy? What monuments are to be toppled? If I go for any throat it is my own.

HE WORRIES about falling asleep lest he miss the six-thirty reporting time. The insomnia of the condemned. Dawn; firing squads, the bucolic clearings of duelers; dawn, the scaffold, the gibbet, the guillotine. Brian waits with the assassin, the suicide, the convict, each with his thoughts. The night holds; a siren wails, set off in a parked car. A Spanish song is being played over and over down the street. Brian stares, asks himself again and again: Why don't I know?

He pictures his parents: His father fallen asleep in front of the colored television on which the figures had turned purple. A photograph of his mother in her youth. The bone of her leg prominent, the calf loose behind, the sheen of lisle.

He sees Mrs. Grass ironing, forever ironing, in the dim light of her kitchen. She tells him a story about her obstetrician who, she said, looked like the bulldog he kept. "He heard me mention that one day and vowed to get back at me . . . so during an examination after a delivery—maybe I shouldn't tell you this," she said, looking at him, the earnest nineteen-year-old, "Oh, well," she went on, in sweet vanquished reluctance, "he said, 'Clean as a whistle, just like a brood mare.'"

All those days and nights in her kitchen; Brian shakes

his head in wonderment over the warm hours they shared. Mr. Grass had come in from the living room where he had fallen asleep. "It's just about time to climb the wooden hill," he said to his wife and began to fiddle with the small radio by the sink. A revival program from Texas, looting the abandoned early morning air waves, came on. A boy soprano sang: "Nothing between my soul and my Saviour/So His Blessed face may be seen/Nothing preventing the least of His favor . . ."

"Oh, shut it off, Abe," Mrs. Grass said to her husband, "It makes me so melancholy."

BRIAN IS capable of being a soldier; capable of being a prisoner; either choice is odious to him. How incontinent this country is to those who fill its graves; the only solace it offers is that more will follow. "You will not be the last!" cry the statues in the parks.

He goes to look at the boil which had erupted on his back. That night he dreamt that a coffee can was squeezed out of his back, full of loam and white worms. He touches the sore and white substance, curd shoots out. Thin red blood bubbles behind. I should have gone to a doctor, he thinks. It will heal badly. Will the medical examiners take someone with boils? he wonders ruefully.

The night: blood, pus, boils. The cockroaches are more decisive than I, Brian says to himself, watching them wag their feelers. He is disgusted with this search of his person, trying to find something that would make him unfit. His gums bleed occasionally; he leaves red crescents on soft white bread. Jake's lanky body had been hewn with effort; and I? he considers. Pasty, soft flesh, bleeding gums, the exploded boil on my back. I fight against the army because it pulls me towards it. A vice; easing into the regimentation, bed and board, spending money, savings bonds. I'm tempted; go, make the best of it; you can adjust to anything.

Jake's motions had been oiled with confidence. He could convince you to sign any dark contract; you do that with the devil, not the damned. Jake survived. Call up the dead, those torn asunder. Jake is the temptation; he is mortality's rebuke. The burnished soul, the perfect piece. Jake has an aura; cloaked with power. The warrior, the transformed man.

Jake's snapshots of him and others sitting atop a blasted knoll; the tops of the hills sheared of foliage like a monk's shaved pate. Bored gladiators, banished from the arena into the jungles. Lost in time, drifting from century to century, caught in the backwaters of a history that flooded its borders. Jake had flipped through the photographs like a gypsy with fortune-telling cards. He and his buddies in the green hills of Vietnam; LZ Moriah. Left there by an overwhelming tide, sudden and inexplicable to them, either a freak of nature or as predictable as the Nile's breaching of its banks. Boys from the fertile underbelly of the country; left there, puzzled, desperate, annoyed, then calm. A shark caught in a tidal pool, after furiously testing his lot, decides there is naught to do, that he is indeed trapped and may die. When exhaustion becomes profound it turns into resignation. And that was their look.

Jake, as a medic, placed himself between the soldier and the pacifist; he needn't be either. A healer and in this instance he could heal himself. Spared the single-mindedness of the foot soldier, the double life of Vietnam, split between itself and the world, he could achieve a resolution, since his life too was doubled.

Twelve months at war and he was not sure if he killed anyone. When you encounter the enemy, he had said, they were told, pull back and call in the artillery. Air power. They served as beaters, slaves of the white hunters, making a din to flush out the quarry. Pull back and call in the artillery.

And his year there. One twelve-month period. Anything can be endured for a year. Even madness. Time reigns, the calendar becomes a bet, the odds increase each day. Three hundred sixty-five-to-one. Three hundred sixty-four-to-one. Vietnam was a state, grown over in the mind like the nervous excretion of an oyster, pearling its irritant, in readiness to be expelled, or lived with: rounded, the most comfortable shape. Vietnam: 12 months, 365 days, 52 weeks, four seasons, a single circumscription of the sun—rounded.

It is easier, Brian knew, to answer for an action taken, than one not attempted. With any broken pot there comes an excuse. But what is there for the extended hand withheld, the unoffered response, for doing nothing? Why didn't you? is the shrill question for which there is no adequate reply. We often do things in order not to explain why we didn't.

If the war goes on much longer, Jake had said, some of the Viet Cong we will be shooting will be half-American.

What wild acts will be committed out of fear? Fear glimpsed on the farthest arc of peripheral vision, where pain gains shape, is infused with possibility, made ambulatory by chance. Fear. Loss of life. Like any vision it cannot be long sustained. I am not afraid. I am willing to take chances, accept statistics, odds, probability. Chance polices fear. Chance is the inviolate space between possibility. Fear. You live with it as you do intestinal parasites.

A TRICKLE of blood runs down his back; he stares, focusing nowhere, the Spanish song a distant, incomprehensible voice, waiting for dawn. He falls into lust's sharp lassitude, begins to imagine Audrey. Had he been a painter and the oils daubed so poorly he would have put aside his brushes; had he been a sculptor and found the clay so unyielding he would have ceased, but being none of those he kept on. He wonders now if she is sleeping with someone at this moment; the memories that vex most are the imagined sexual acts of others.

She was so unlike me and that is why I thirsted for her,

he tells himself; she seemed to be a Canaan beyond the Dead Sea of the draft. What worried her? Telling about her life, the men she had known, flashes of violence, a blow struck on the George Washington Bridge, her red blood on a white dress. She withheld and implied details; they had the stuff of dreams about them. He became as entangled as she in the tendrils of her past. Never married, thirty, childless. Affairs, each afflicted with the same pattern. He was not usual for her, but neither did he solve anything; by being not cut from her same cloth, but an odd patch, he set her predicament more clearly in her mind. He confirmed her own loneliness and she his. His life had been cinched by the draft, forced to narrow, but Audrey's? His fate had been institutionalized, but hers is less distinct. The army she could resist or join is traditional too; some liberty would be lost, but with it certain fears.

How did she think of herself? Witchy, thin-lipped, easily afraid, a voice tremulous at the start, that took a few sentences to become smooth, gain confidence. Her beauty increased the size of every possible disappointment; yet in it there was comfort. It would bring a silent smile to her face on occasion, as if she was having an especially pleasant memory.

She faced her own dilemma, Brian recognized. But why did she let me spend so much time with her, he kept asking himself, but no longer let me touch her? All the nights he had walked back to his room from her apartment, banished, shut out, sent away; teeth clenched, the terrible mix he had swallowed, served in a vial of rejection—tenderness transformed into rage, his face a menacing mask. He never had a lover's hours with her that can be as languorous as a swan's neck. So much time had been spent in piercing her reluctance. And then. Nothing. There was so much to discover; he knew as much about his body as his right hand had taught him, but she had shut herself.

"You know, sex can be delightful with someone else, besides myself," she had said to him. She would not allow him to root for she knows they can go into her as deep as a fig tree's.

He smiles at the recollection of her love-potion Bryn Mawr meals. He was little but powerfully affected. She had no sour smell of want or any dullness of neglect. Her limbs were not gnarled by work, her smooth blondeness spoke of effortless perfection, the warmth of flame. She was ease, vanquished toil, thoughtless health, preciously educated. Audrey was the idolators' calf, the hammered icon, the encrusted shell. She tapped hidden springs, the gold fever of conquerers and kings. Her blondeness marked her for sacrifice; she would be an object, revered without wish, named angel, thought spotless, unsoiled. Most desirable, most defilable, flesh temple of blasphemers, sport of myth, result of mind-panning, the sifting out of dross—blonde, fair, symbol of greed, the golden fang of avarice. If there was a flaw in her surface it was her eyes. They emitted question, betrayed the shell centuries of refining had been finishing. The eyes would not blandly acquiesce; they would protest, and if with nothing else, then with the blankness of the beauty that is rendered in marble. I am something else, they would complain. Not needing to be more than she was she allowed herself to be less, and she was now aware that the inertia of her blondeness, the culture that held her image up, adored it, made way for it, had begun to close behind her, almost cutting off the retreat she was just beginning to make.

Life had been easy, but now it began to harden. She neglected to win, to pick up the prizes early offered. The race is done and she has dozed. She wakes in the damp dusk, the crowds have gone, the pennants fallen, all have been trampled beneath departing feet.

We pursue those who reveal our faults, whose gaze is the harshest light; who then, by their continuing presence, atone for our imperfections. This boiling off of our failings, under the heat of their attention, is what is longed for; we look for purification, those who can work this alchemy, changing our baseness.

If we do not touch squalid depths in others we cannot hope to win them. They will always be skittish, worry that the façade will crack, that his or her estimation will suddenly change. A person will be degraded in the eyes of another in order to find their bedrock. Degrade. Earth, stripped layer by layer, each grade removed till bedrock is reached. Brian made the mistake of appealing to Audrey's virtues and strengths and not her vices and weaknesses and that only makes a person uncomfortable.

HIS THOUGHTS, the only companions which keep him company, finally drop off drossily; he stirs them, they fade again. A man will even hoard misery if it is the last of his possessions. And Brian embraces his woe. He is troubled that even now he is still plagued with images of Audrey. Though, even at death, the last sense to be given-up is touch; the hands of the unconscious are still tightly held.

He knows she is lost to him. And when you lose a woman you know you could have loved, the discovery of that knowledge is like finding the costly gold setting of a ring that is missing its stone. Difficult to throw away, you keep it, though you are never quite sure why.

EIGHTEEN

Vigils end. Candles leave their hoary stumps; every event has its dark fruition. He wonders what to wear; who will collect his belongings from the room? Will I be able to make calls? He reads the directions to Whitehall Street again. A change of subways. South Ferry. He has never gone there. He takes up the induction order and the pink envelope and leaves. He looks upon the leperous walls of the hallway fondly; he has grown used to the tomb, affectionate towards the cerecloth.

The stores of Seventy-second Street are shut, single lights burn, the sacristy lamps of commerce. Sheets of newsprint scud along the street. The day slumbers; but beneath the pavement, the subways are full; there people list against the dawn.

He enters a car, the eyes dip over him like fingers in holy water, a split-second benediction. You can tell the time by their clothes; these are the people who open doors, sweep away the night's debris; they are the dour scouts who break camp.

In another hour the cars will fill with the second wave; officers emerging from their tents, physicians reaching for arrayed knives, patrons sitting at prepared tables, subalterns filling baskets that have just been emptied. The men and women sit in the subway car impassively, braced with acceptance.

The car smells of things of the night. The iron shrieks; passengers are hushed before it, silenced by its rage. The roar fills his head; he clasps his hands over his ears; the tumult becomes musical, distant, shelled. Brian thinks he's truly going mad. This caravan of stoics, rigid with compliance, in free-fall, stiffened to receive the impending blow, the look of passengers before a crash—startled into primness.

Brian looks up: The long sonorous wail is accompanied. A blind saxaphone player plies his way down the careening aisle, a tin cup tied to the shank of the instrument. A dirge of machinery, deep hollow notes; his flaccid eyelids do not grip, though the rest of his face is constricted with his efforts.

Each stop is a frieze of humiliation. Fates' hostages, nonce companions, fraternity of coincidence, they continue towards Whitehall Street, through the underground city of Dis.

The doors shudder open and he steps onto the cement

causeway of Chambers Street to change for the local. There is a page of the induction order that is to be filled out before arriving, and he begins to fill in the blanks with a stub of a pencil. His father's and mother's names. He cannot go beyond them. Writing their names is the first courtyard denial. Surrounded by cement and iron, crusted black dirt, carapace of hard use, with the morning shades ready to cross over, tokens touching their lips, the first acid taste of the bleached night. A local rumbles in: SOUTH FERRY. They board.

DECAYING WATERFRONT, the land's uneasy edge, thickens the air with the odors of putrefaction. Brian asks the way to the Induction Center and a man points silently. A squat brick building, with small archways, fast by the boundary of a park.

Uniforms, posters, hand-lettered signs. Two soldiers stand in front of an ornate cage. An elevator no longer in use. They point to the stairway behind it. No one has spoken to him since he left. Terminal gestures, final destinations, the lifted arm, the extended finger, the solemnity of indication.

A scattered number of young men squat on risers. Sports bleachers, small-town playing fields. There are not many here; it is a special day that inducts only transfers.

There are fewer men here than states; listening to the names of the towns they come from is to hear a recitation from a world atlas. This union's transients; they are a mixed lot, hybrid by traveling.

A black sergeant talks about lunch passes; he hands out slips of paper upon which to mark a preference: army or marines. Catcalls greet the choice.

"And, if anyone of you is going to refuse induction, let us know now," he says and yawns; it bores him. No one stirs.

Brian had gone with Jake the day of his induction. The Armed Forces Building in their hometown had the same transfer-point air, a place of interim, a state of half-life, everyone thought of beyond. Jake had entered a world of men who knew they were to be together and the slow sifting of acquaintanceship began. Sized up. Twenty years old; so much had prepared them for it. As young men protested the war after vicariously sampling its savagery, seeing burning flesh, the capricious mayhem, the macabre wantonness of their tasks, had felt, tasted, basked in its death, others had learned best to live with it, became toughened to its cutting edge. Severed heads, ovens caked with bodies, lime-coated pits, the atomic annulment of men to shadows, all this they had seen and it did not stop them; no generation had been better prepared for war, or worse. Ours is essentially a grotesque age and therefore nothing that occurs seems particularly bizarre. Jake quickly became an acting sergeant; his stripes were on a black mourning band tied around his arm. He said he had been picked because of his height.

An ear a day keeps the Gooks away, Brian remembered. This sore must be lanced, he knew, and this squat brick building would be the dull blade that does it. There are signs on the walls; his eyes wipe over them like a greasy rag across glass.

> THE SECURITY
> OF THE WORLD
> BEGINS HERE

They file into another room and begin to fill in forms. There is a long checklist, a medical history, diseases, infirmities; near the bottom: *homosexual tendencies*. He marks it. The soldier who checks the papers signs a slip and without looking up says, "Go to Room 302."

Corridors, frosted snowflake glass, green rooms. Brian had been expecting crowds; there is no one waiting. He stands in the doorway with his file in his hand. There are two desks; behind each is what he takes to be psychiatrists. At the front desk a young man sits. His hair is coiffured and streaked; he wears make-up and a belt made out of large gold rings. The man who interviews him wears a bright blue blazer, a ruddy face smiling a Chamber of Commerce grin. They chat amicably. Brian thinks: This is not going to work.

A tiny man sits at the other desk, bent over, scratching notations. A few fingers of hair cover his head. He is over sixty, East European; his clothing is nondescript. He motions to Brian and he takes the seat offered. Brian hands him the file which he studies; when he begins to speak Brian hands him the sealed letter. Every terrible act is accomplished with a familiar gesture. A trigger squeezed, a club arched, a knife shoved forward, a cheek kissed. Brian hands him the letter; he takes it. The arc is completed; the infection passed.

He reads and his frown deepens. His face is tight, pensive flesh; he is fatigued, irritated. He is here only temporarily, on a day-to-day basis. Brian wonders if he needs the money.

"There was nothing like this mentioned at your first physical, three years ago, which qualified you 1-A."

"That took place in my hometown and I didn't want it to come out," Brian says, deceit as plausible as truth.

"Are you an active or passive homosexual?"

Brian does not know what that entails; but thinks it best to be positive, claim action.

"Is there any history of mental illness in your family? I see it's checked . . ."

He had checked everything as he had been advised.

"Well," Brian says, searching, "my grandmother was senile . . ."

"Senility is a condition of aging and not a mental illness," he snaps.

"How long have you been seeing this doctor?" he says, turning back the first page of the letter like a bed sheet.

Brian shrugs, finding it physically difficult to continue to dissemble; he no longer has the voice for it, even his body begins to harden against it.

The doctor asks his colleague for a book; he needs to look up codes and formulae; he is not familiar with the procedures. The other man gives his an explanation of the paper work. Could this be his first day here? Brian thinks. What if I had drawn the man with the Chamber of Commerce smile?

The doctor regards him; Brian looks stricken; he cannot feel himself to reflect anything but that. It is an honest expression, but how would it be interpreted? Would it pass, reflect whatever had been written in the letter?

Brian fights back wanting to get up and leave, wanting to shout: FUCK THIS SHIT! COUNT ME OUT! I DECIDE. I CHOOSE. AND I DECLINE.

He does nothing; he sits. A solitary man, it has been proposed, could move the earth given a fulcrum of sufficient size; yet it took the entire earth and that fulcrum, the war, to move Brian. The weight of it; yet it still barely tips his scales. Had there been fewer reasons he could never have put himself through this; he would have succumbed.

The physician looks at Brian and Brian does not know what he sees. His life has seen more pain than Brian's. It has worn away his face; he is a superintendent of suffering. His accent places him in Europe before the World War, One or Two, or both. He stares at Brian a passing moment. His thin gray head is a ruin, his eyes black windows, his breathing the acrid whisps of smoke trailing down battered alleys; his lips slightly curl, no more than wind indenting dust. The physician's is the wizened face that stares out from huddled crowds: victim. One who endures. His expression is one of suffering and scorn: the face of an eternally lingering illness.

Brian refuses the legacy and he thinks him ungrateful. The bondage of pain is recognized by all and Brian is forefeiting his birthright, the right to mourn. It is what men ask of each other; to die in order that others may live.

The green room, the desk and chair, this test, an initiation, a rite of passage. A crossing-over has been made, a ceremony as complete as any dance with painted faces, shrieks in the night, flaming torches, narcotic smoke. The old man stares reproachfully at Brian. Have I failed him, failed myself?

He hands Brian his folder, tells him another room number and dismisses him.

NINETEEN

Large windows are glazed and on them appear silhouettes of seagulls. Caws fill the room. The birds' black shadows flap against the whitewashed glass. It is the final examination room. Brian has been jumped ahead; he waits alone. He has another sealed envelope and a new code number penciled atop his file. Dust, thick as summer pollen, drifts through buttressing shafts of light. The only sounds are the sea ravens' voracious caws. They wave, black banners, on the windows.

A dozen youths enter from the rear, loud and mocking, made raucous by the momentum of their morning. They are in various stages of dress, in a state of unexpected flight. Army physicians break into the room from a door in front.

"All right you men strip and spread your cheeks . . ."

They pass by the naked row. For a moment it seems incredibly important. The men step back into their clothes after the examiners leave.

A boy enters the room hesitantly and sits down on the other end of the bench Brian occupies. He appears younger than the eighteen he must be. Puerto Rican. He wears poor, tight fitting clothes; thin and emaciated, he is weaker than a reed. His wiry hair is slicked back in an elaborate style. It looks like the tarred wing of a bird. There are a few Puerto Ricans in the larger group and they begin to taunt the boy.

"Hey, señorita," they lilt, "Carmencita!"

"Ooo, la la!"

They begin to dance with each other, roll their eyes, laugh and swivel their hips in the direction of the boy.

"Muy linda, señorita . . ."

The boy does not look at them; he starts to cry. The tear makes a bright path down his face, a finger tracing along a dusty tabletop.

The jeers continue. If he had been an insect they would have torn his legs off. Rebukes swirl around his head.

What a different story his must be, Brian thinks, that puts him here; nonetheless we cross. He wonders if the boy's tears are the least significant to be spilt because of the war. How long its reach. All the young men it has touched know the meekness of Isaac as he waited beneath his father's knife.

The boy continues to weep, muddying his cheeks.

Insults come till the doctors return; then they stop as if it is an interrupted song.

Processing continues; more men file into the room; additional marks are made on Brian's papers.

"You are completely unfit for service in the Armed Forces," a young soldier tells Brian, "you will be sent your 4-F classification by your local draft board."

Brian leaves the building and the sunlight stuns him, shuts his eyes; all he senses is the waterfront's decay. He opens his mouth as if to offer an explanation but no sound comes forth. Nothing, nothing, nothing, nothing, nothing.

EPILOGUE

This thought is as a death, which cannot choose
But weep to have that which it fears to lose.
—Shakespeare, *Sonnet LXIV*

BRIAN WAS freed from the draft, but it was not so much a release as an absence, not beneficial, but desultory, and so ungirded, he fell like the son of Daedalus toward the sea, the Gulf of Mexico.

A change of compass is often marked by new geography; Brian was able to meet Jake and his bride in New Orleans. They discovered an old school friend who was singing at the Bayou Club. He greeted Jake: "Hey, man, I thought you had ended up in a ditch in Nam."

The next morning, Easter Sunday, carriages broken out in flowers rolled through the French Quarter; people went off to church in finery bright as a spinning coin.

The following day they left, driving back to the

Midwest. Dead trees hung with goat beards of Spanish moss. They passed through a tired Mississippi hamlet. A trash fire burned behind a tar paper shack.

"That's *exactly* what a Gook village smells like," Jake said.

Jerry-built strawberry wine stands dot Highway 51. Odd, unmatched bottles filled with red wine; they flash in the sun like mounted garnets.

"Strawberry plasma stands," Jake says, "we ought to buy a bottle or two; just what we survivors need." They share dark laughter.

No matter what decision Brian made he knew he would be injured; it was a choice of not picking the wound, but deciding on the scar. Or so he told himself.

They drive through the damp southern night and reach the heartland at daybreak. Tractors move lugubriously along the roadside, their small front tires wobbling pigeon-toed. Fields have been harrowed and the troughs glow with hoarfrost.

"You know what a dead skunk smells like?" Jake says. Flattened skunks blotch the macadam. The car fills with their ripe rot. "It smells like a box of new balloons."